Missed Exit
A Poorly Navigated Romantic Comedy

Indie Sparks

Indie Sparks

Twice Shy Publishing

Copyright © 2025 by Indie Sparks

All rights reserved.

No part of this publication may be reproduced, distributed, or transmitted in any form or by any means, including photocopying, recording, or other electronic or mechanical methods, without the prior written permission of the publisher, except as permitted by U.S. copyright law.

No part of this book may be used to create, feed, or refine artificial intelligence models, for any purpose, without written permission from the author. For permission requests, please contact: twiceshypub@yahoo.com or sparksbyindie@gmail.com

The story, all names, characters, and incidents portrayed in this production are fictitious, created without use of AI technology. No identification with actual persons (living or deceased), places, buildings, and products is intended or should be inferred. This book is a work of fiction meant to entertain only, and as such, no part of this story should be interpreted as instructional or as any form of professional advice.

Book Cover by Indie Sparks

Edited by Beth Hudson Ink

Print ISBN: 979-8-9923061-2-5

Sometimes, the detours create the best memories.

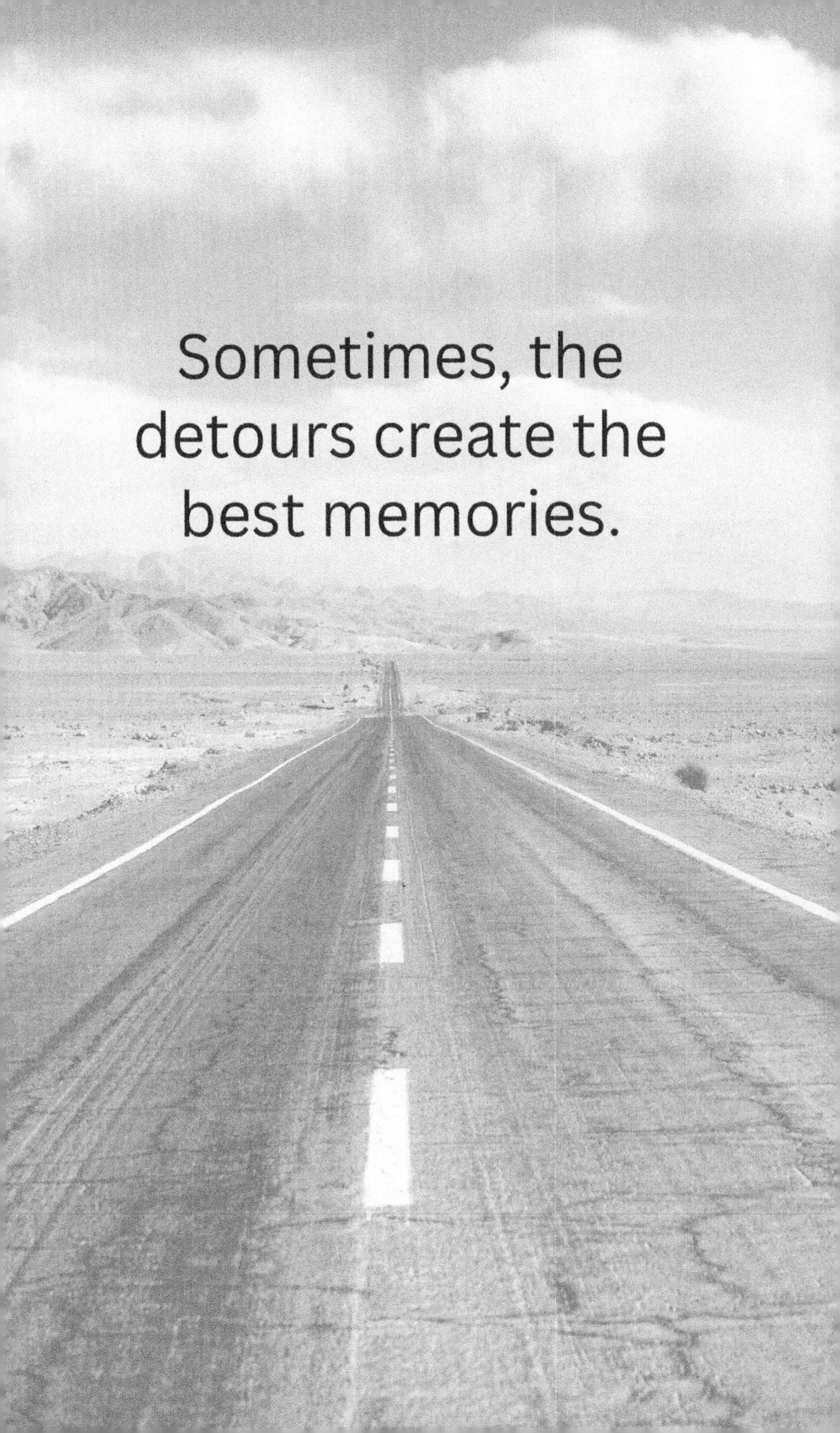

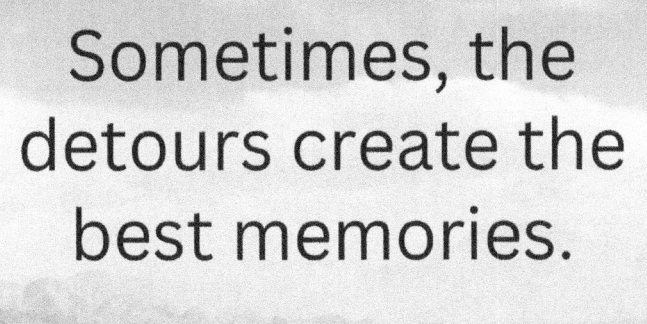

1

Greta

I Hope His Tailgate Falls Off

I shake my head to ward off the highway hypnosis. It happens so easily out here in the middle of nowhere, but I'm too close to my destination to stop now. And I've come too far to doze off at the wheel and wake up in the afterlife with some angel narrating the highlights of my life story—especially the last chapter.

Thanks, but no thanks. Been there. Done that. Have the emotional scars to prove it.

Another shake of my head and downing the dregs of my now very warm, watered-down cold brew wakes me back up. Whoa, that's bitter. Me and my coffee: both bitter and past our prime.

Slipping back into self-pity-mode is exactly what I promised my therapist I wasn't going to do . . . right after I promised her I wasn't going to run away from my problems.

What does she know, anyway?

She wouldn't answer when I asked the question—just gave me that astonished look she gives for a hundred and fifty bucks an hour—but I'm sure she never had a fiancé confess that he's been fucking his brother's wife the day after her wedding planner mailed their invitations. She and I are not the same.

And since she's never been through it, she doesn't actually have a clue what I'm dealing with.

It's been six weeks since the bomb went off, and I still get messages every time someone new finds out the wedding is off. They all start off sympathetic and caring, but quickly slide right into the prying questions.

The bastard could've at least done me the favor of imploding our fairytale one day sooner.

Okay, maybe we weren't exactly living a modern-day fairytale, but his timing added insult to injury.

It's not like you can call back your mail from the US Postal Service. Don't even ask. Begging won't work either. And they're immune to the tears of a broken-hearted public-school teacher.

As if we don't have enough reason to cry every damn day without having our hearts shattered by an architect named Brick, who's been extremely devoted to a very important project for going on six months now. So much overtime. So many out-of-town visits to the building site.

Yes, really. On both counts—his name and his behavior.

Clearly, I'm not so great with initial clues. Or apparently, any clues thereafter. Because I'm told there were additional clues. Did my friends bother to tell me when they saw those clues?

To be fair, Carter insists that she did, but I wasn't ready to hear it.

So, I made excuses for him.

I vaguely recall a few conversations where that might have happened. A lot of my memories are vague right now, sort of like ruined watercolors where all you can make out are browns and grays and pukey greens all smeared together.

What's done is done, though. And I'm done with my sad, ugly memories.

But I'm not running away; just hitting the reset button. Six months in Agate Ridge, Texas—miles and miles from Brick the Dick. That's his name now. Anyway, this little break from crisis should be plenty of time to heal my heart and put me back on track.

One thing's for sure: I won't run into anyone I know. And that is exactly the way I want it. I'll be a stranger in a strange place.

I won't even bother to meet my neighbors. In fact, I'll avoid them at all costs. This is my hermit era, and nobody is going to ruin it for me. I've earned this shit.

A new crop of cars appears in my rearview mirror. It's been like this for the entire seven-hour drive. Clumps of traffic and then miles of near isolation. I prefer the latter, but I know we're getting close to Agate Ridge. It's the farthest west exit for a string of small towns right off I-10, the last populated patch before another long stretch of nothing.

I'll be far from any bustling cities, but there's enough of a population to warrant a small grocery store and emergency services. And those were just about my only requirements, so it'll be perfect.

I watch as a bigger vehicle breaks away from the pack behind me. It's coming up fast, so I move into the right lane. My exit shouldn't be too far ahead, anyway.

Oh, not this asshole again!

This wannabe cowboy in his big, black pickup truck made my drive hell for nearly two hours. I thought he turned off miles ago. Right after I let my middle finger do the talking.

Shit. I'm not sure I want this guy to catch up to me again. Maybe he changed his mind about letting me get the last word, or in our case, the final gesture.

He could be crazy. He could be dangerous!

I floor it, but my car struggles with the command. The acceleration has been shit since about an hour this side of Austin, but she's basically running fine once she's up to speed. Just takes her a little while to get up and go, that's all.

Why isn't she getting up and going right now? Is she slowing down? She's dying? No, no, no, no, no . . . not when I've got a raging psychopath on my ass!

Finally, my engine gets the message and the RPMs start to climb. Yes!

Not today, you revenge-seeking redneck!

I honk my horn as I blow past him. He immediately moves over into the right lane behind me. Is he going to follow me now? Uh-oh. Maybe I honked too soon.

Nope. I'm safe. He just moved over to exit again. Can't make up his mind where he's going, apparently. Or maybe he didn't want to chance it. For all he knows, I could be the crazy one. I could be dangerous!

"Chicken!" I yell as I watch him in my passenger side mirror, cruising away from the interstate. "What's the matter? Afraid of little ole me in my little red car? Not so big and bad after all, are you?" I laugh as he fades out of sight.

Ahhh, good times. Even during the darkest of days, there's always something to laugh about.

That's exactly the kind of bullshit I used to say to my middle schoolers, but sometimes, there's a little truth buried in the bullshit.

And if I can laugh on my way to a rented duplex in the ass crack of west Texas with a broken engagement, no job to go back to when school starts, and my dignity in the gutter . . . well, sometimes all you can do is laugh.

Even when you realize every important choice you've ever made has been total bullshit.

But I'm done with that life. It's firmly in my rearview mirror, and I'm forging ahead.

Fuuuuuuck!

The exit for Agate Ridge is literally in my rearview right now.

There is nothing ahead but wide-open road. For miles and miles . . .

I'm supposed to meet the moving truck in an hour, and that asshole took my exit!

It's fine. Everything's fine. There is no need to catastrophize the situation. I'll just take the next exit and circle back around.

This is simply a minor delay, not a major complication. I've got this.

New, uncomplicated life, here I come!

2
Law

Howdy, Neighbor

When I started this beer, I decided if my new neighbor ended up being a no-show, I'd take the TV, and then I'd call the landlord to let him know his new tenant left all their shit on the driveway but they don't appear to be moving in.

As I sit here, rocking in my porch swing and finishing off my second beer, I've already faced the fact that I'm not going to take a damn thing those pissed off movers left behind.

I do need a new TV, and that's a nice one sitting on the other half of the driveway next to my truck, but I'm no thief. I might be a lot of things, but I am not a thief.

Plenty of people steal in all sorts of ways and do just fine. Some become millionaires. Billionaires, even. But I'm not made that way. Never have been.

And what's it gotten me? A rented duplex and a TV with a blurry stripe running through the middle of the screen. Most movies are still watchable. Makes a ballgame hard to follow, though.

Where the hell is this person who failed to meet their movers? I hope they're okay.

My curiosity gets the best of me, so I walk over to take a closer look at their things.

Even through multiple layers of bubble wrap, I can tell that's got to be an 85-inch screen. Did he not take any measurements of this place? That TV is going to cover an entire wall in his living room. He'll have to watch it from the kitchen.

The couch is awfully small. Doesn't go with the TV. Weird. You'd think a guy who cared so much about the size of his TV would at least have a nice, leather recliner.

I'm glad to see his headboard is solid wood. He even has a footboard. This is a sturdy looking bed. Hopefully, that means I won't have to hear it banging against our shared wall.

The last guy who lived here was okay as far as neighbors go, but the thumping rhythm of his revolving-door love life was a constant reminder that mine paled in comparison.

Not that I'm making much of an effort in that area these days, but I don't need a nightly confirmation.

In his defense, he did move his bed away from the wall after I offered to come over and add a few screws to shore up his headboard. He got a good laugh out of the offer. And an ego boost, I'm sure. At least I could get a full night's sleep for the last few months he was here.

I hope this new neighbor doesn't make me miss that guy.

I've seen enough. He'll either show up or he won't.

I push my front door open, but before I can step inside, tires roll to a stop at the curb. When I turn to see who's pulled up, I don't recognize the car. This has got to be my new neighbor.

I've already stood here staring, so it would be rude not to wait a bit longer and introduce myself.

A passenger emerges from the backseat, and soon as she stands up, our eyes lock.

Oh, come on! What are the fucking odds? This whole life must be my penance for all the bad shit I did in a past life.

Her head swivels repeatedly, looking at all her belongings exposed for the whole world to inspect, but it comes to a full stop when she recognizes my truck. The shock in her expression is almost comical.

"Where's your little red race car?" I call out.

"It died." She paces alongside the driveway as her ride pulls away. "They just unloaded all my stuff and left it here?"

"They waited about thirty minutes before they gave up on you. Did you get lost?"

"No. I did not get lost. You made me miss my exit! And then my car died, so I had to wait on a tow truck, and then I had to wait on a ride. Do you know how long it takes to get an Uber out here?"

"No idea. I also have no idea how you figure I made you miss your exit." I walk to the edge of my porch because I don't think I'm going inside anytime soon. "I took that exit easily enough. What kept you from taking it?"

"You!"

"Yeah, repeating that isn't going to make it true. I had nothing to do with you missing the exit."

"Yes, you did! You, road-raging psychopath!"

"Road rage? What road rage?"

"You tried to intimidate me for miles, and then you came speeding back up on my bumper out of nowhere, practically pushing me out of my lane."

"Do you have a head injury or some other condition that affects your memory? Because I'm about to say some things to you that I would genuinely feel bad for saying to someone with an actual disability."

"Say whatever you want. I don't care what you think about me, anyway!"

"Look, I'm going to go out on a limb here and assume we've both had a bad day. Let's start over." I run my fingers through my hair, and hope I don't regret not walking into my own place and closing the door on her. "Howdy, neighbor. Want some help carrying all your shit inside?"

"Seems like the least you could do at this point."

I inhale for ten. Exhale the entire breath on one. "Listen, I did not make you miss the exit. I also did not make your movers leave. I am offering to help you because I'm a nice guy, not because I owe it to you. I don't owe you anything."

"Fine!"

She bends down to pick up the footboard to her bed. There's no way she can lift that alone. I set my beer bottle on the porch railing and walk toward her. "Hold on. I'll help you with—"

Before I can reach her, she lifts one end of it and starts dragging it across the concrete.

"Stop! That's nice wood. You're going to ruin it. Let me help. Please."

"I flipped you off on the freeway."

"Yes. And I'll cherish the memory, always."

"Because you cut me off."

"I do not remember that part."

"Well, you did."

"I'll take your word for it."

"And?"

"And what?"

"How about an apology?"

"Oh, I guess I thought the part where you flipped me off negated the need for that."

She stares at me, standing her ground with her end of the footboard still raised.

I remind myself that I'm the one who initiated this interaction, so I try again. "You want to tell me your name?"

"Greta. Greta Gaines."

"I am very sorry if I cut you off in traffic, Greta Gaines." I lift the other end of the footboard. "That would be a great stage name, by the way. Sorry. Hazard of the industry."

I take a step forward as she unceremoniously drops her end of the footboard, causing me to stumble into my end. "What the hell? Why did you do that?"

"Did you just insinuate that I'm a stripper?"

"Not in English."

"You said I had a great *stage name*."

"That's not the kind of stage I meant. It's a great name for a singer. Are you a singer, by any chance?"

"No."

"Welp, then congratulations. You've got a good-for-nothing name as far as I can tell. You want to help me move this inside now?"

"Are you going to tell me your name?"

"Law. Law Davis."

"Law?"

"Short for Lawson, but pretty much only my mama calls me that."

"Your mama, huh? You're obviously a Texas boy."

"And with that twang in your voice, you're obviously a Texas girl. After we move all your stuff, we can compare family trees, but if you wouldn't mind—"

"I do not have a *twang*."

"You've got a little twang. And for the record, Greta Gaines would be a terrible stripper name."

"Are you done insulting me?"

"Oh, now it's an insult if you *don't* have a stripper name?"

"I'm only insulted because you think you can make assumptions about me. You don't know me. There's nothing wrong with being a stripper, by the way. Sex workers deserve the same respect as anyone else, but thanks to men—"

"Maybe we should do a little more moving and a whole lot less talking."

She huffs at me, but she lifts her end of the footboard again. She's stronger than she looks, and she's got really pretty eyes, even when they're glaring at me.

I doubt she's going to be any quieter than the last guy who lived here, but I don't think I'm going to miss him at all.

3

Greta

TOO CLOSE FOR COMFORT

Law helps me move all my heavy stuff off the driveway. He even sticks around to help me carry in boxes. Maybe he's not as bad as I thought. But I'm not rushing to judgment. I've only known him a few hours.

"Do you want help putting your bed together?"

"You have tools for that?"

He laughs, and I'm not sure I like the sound of it. "Yeah, I have tools."

"Okay. If I'm not keeping you from anything."

"I've got time to put a bed together before I head out. If you have anything else that requires assembly, you'll have to wait until tomorrow."

"Where are you heading out to?"

"My job."

"You work nights?"

"Mostly. How about you?"

"I'm a school teacher. But I'm on a break. For now, I work here." I look around at my small living room separated from the kitchen by a Formica-topped bar. There is no hallway between the living room and the bedroom, just a door. And to get to the only bathroom, I have to walk through my bedroom, which means any guests I have over will have to do the same.

Not that I plan on having any guests. But this place looks a lot smaller than it did in the pictures.

"What do you mean you work here? As in, right here?"

"People work remotely now. It's not unusual."

"Some people do. But the pandemic's been over for a long time. Are students still attending school remotely?"

"I have some other work to do. I'll be . . . well, I, I write things."

"What kind of things? Like textbooks or something?"

"When you look at me, that's all you think I'd be capable of writing? Textbooks?"

"You said you were a school teacher, so I assumed if you were writing . . . forget it. I'll just put your bed together and get out of your way."

"I have to show you where I want it first."

"There's only one wall with enough room." He walks into my bedroom like he owns the place. I follow him. He points at the wall with the living room on the other side. "That wall has a door in the middle. That one has a window in the middle, and that one has your closet door and your bathroom door on it, so you really only have one option."

He nods toward the only wall with enough open space to put a bed against it.

"Is your side of the duplex the same layout?"

"Yep."

"Is your headboard on the other side of that wall?"

"Sure is."

"Our headboards have to be back-to-back?"

"My bed's not right up against the wall, and yours doesn't have to be either. I promise I will ensure the maximum amount of space between our heads."

"Good. I don't want to hear you snoring through the wall."

"You sure that's what you're worried about hearing?" He smirks, leaning against my bathroom door.

"Can you just go get your tools, please?"

When he leaves, I listen for the sounds of him entering his side of the duplex. I can hear his front door open and close, but I don't hear him walking around inside. Good. I want to be as insulated from his life as possible.

It's bad enough he works nights, so I'll probably hear him coming home at a ridiculously early hour every morning. The last thing I need is a sunrise soundtrack of whatever he does before he falls asleep, alone or with a partner. I don't want to know.

I hear the faint but unmistakable sound of his toilet flushing. Ugh. At least I couldn't hear him peeing.

A sudden image of him standing in his bathroom with his fly open flashes in my mind. I squeeze my eyes shut to keep from imagining his hand or what it's probably tucking back into his underwear right now . . . but apparently, mental images don't care if your eyes are open or not.

Why would my brain go there? I don't want to see his dick. Is that where his brain is going to go if he hears me flush my toilet? Or turn on my shower?

Oh, God. I don't want this guy imagining me naked every time he hears water running on my side of the wall. I'll have to shower at night while he's at work. But I like morning showers.

I just moved in, and my neighbor is already a problem.

It's not like I should be surprised. He was a problem before I ever knew we were neighbors. I didn't move all this way to wind up stuck with another man who causes problems in my life.

My front door opens. He didn't even knock.

Who the hell does Law Davis think he is?

He strides back into my bedroom, holding a drill and a small plastic box that I know probably has drill bits in it. I'm not entirely clueless. His arm lifts to confirm he's ready to get to work, but my eyes go in an entirely different direction.

I might've given up on therapy too soon. I'm clearly unwell.

But he fills out those jeans quite well. The way the denim hugs his thighs, and the waistband sits so perfectly snug that I'd have to work to get that button undone . . . and I can't even pretend I didn't check out his ass earlier when I was walking behind him.

Who am I? Say something. Don't just stand here, staring at him.

"Looks like you definitely have the right tool to get the job done."

Seriously? That's what came out of my mouth?

It slipped out while my brain was engaged in mental combat with my eyes, trying to keep them out of enemy territory.

Dicks are the enemy, I remind myself. They're bad, and everything attached to them is bad.

I manage to force my eyes up to the drill in his hand, hoping to confirm that's the only tool I was referring to. This all feels so awkward and obvious, but I'm sure it's one of those moments where you think everyone else is noticing something, but you find out later that they weren't paying a bit of attention. It was all in your head.

This is all in my head.

Which is exactly where the image of his dick originally came from. Of course, it wasn't really his dick because I've never seen that part of him, except through his pants. Not that I have x-ray vision. I mean, I can't actually see through his pants—

Oh, God. Now I'm looping:

Imagine his dick. Look in its general direction. Peel your eyes away. Tell yourself you absolutely do not want to see that. Clearly see an image of it in your head again. Catch yourself staring at its zipped-up fort. Force your eyes—

I shake my head. "Sorry. I've had a lot of caffeine today. It makes me a little spacey if I have too much."

"How long was your drive?"

"Seven hours."

"What are you running away from?" He examines the screws in the little bag the movers taped to my headboard, and then he opens his little plastic box and chooses a drill bit.

"Nothing. I just needed some peace and quiet for a while." I help him set the headboard into position, centered on the wall, but about four inches away from it.

"Ah, a change of scenery before the new school year starts, huh? You here for the whole summer?"

"I'm here until Christmas break. At least."

"So, you're taking a semester off?"

"At least."

"Got it."

We work in silence until the bed is whole again. He uses head nods and hand signals to let me know if he needs me to move anything. I'm weirdly grateful he's stopped talking. Stopped asking questions.

"What exactly do you do?" I ask as we hoist my mattress into place. My own curiosity can only take so much silence.

"What's your best guess?"

"Oil field, probably."

"Sweetheart, if I was working in the oil field, I'd be able to afford a much nicer place."

I normally hate when men call me sweetheart, but there's something so unassuming in the way he says it, no discernible condescension to piss me off, so he gets a free pass. This time.

"Well, I know that's an expensive truck you're driving, so you're probably not asking people if they want fries with that."

He laughs, and I can tell I've caught him off guard. I guess he didn't expect me to have a sense of humor. Rude.

"I'm an A & R rep," he says, as if that answers my question.

"Okay, I give up. Does that mean you do legal work for the oil industry?"

"Again, if I was a lawyer for the oil industry—"

"We wouldn't be neighbors."

"Exactly. A & R stands for artists and repertoire. The industry is music."

I stare at him, waiting for him to continue his explanation because I still have no idea what he does.

"Would you recognize the phrase talent scout?"

"Really? Wow. That must be an interesting job."

"It has its moments."

The downside hits me. "That's why you work nights. You have to go where the music is."

"That's the reason."

"Great. You get paid to hang out in bars." I don't mean to scoff out loud, but it's not like I can take it back.

"Does this mean you're constantly bringing home drunk women at the end of your shifts?"

"I'm usually limited to one. On a really good night, maybe—"

"You know what I meant."

"I am a grown man. I may, on occasion, have company, yes. Have you taken a vow of celibacy?"

His tone conveys the indoor equivalent of road rage. Bedroom rage? I almost laugh at that . . . until I realize my brain is drafting a whole new unwelcome image.

"No, I'm not necessarily committed to celibacy, but your kind aren't my favorite people right now."

"A & R?"

"Men."

"I see."

I refuse to look at any part of him now. "I'll buy earplugs."

"So will I." He puts his drill bit back in the box.

"Trust me, you won't need them. I plan on remaining single."

"Yeah, but those battery-operated boyfriends make the worst sounds. That constant whining noise that gets louder and softer and louder and softer and louder and—"

"What are you, twelve?"

"Oh, come on. My sense of humor is at least fifteen."

"You mean *at most*?"

"Welcome to Agate Ridge, Greta." He makes it almost to my front door before he turns abruptly and says, "Wait. Do you write porn? Is that why you got so cagey about it?"

"I did not get cagey. And no, I don't write porn. Do I look like I write porn?"

He actually narrows his eyes and give me an up-down visual inspection. "I don't know. I've never met a porn writer, so I have no idea what y'all might look like."

"You mean as far as you know, you've never met one. You can't be sure."

His eyebrows lift, along with the corners of his mouth. "Good point. Enjoy the writin'."

"Enjoy the scoutin'. And thanks for your help."

"You know, a truly grateful neighbor might thank me with freshly baked cookies."

"If you're lucky, maybe I'll buy you a bag of chips."

"Not a baker. Noted."

He walks out, and I watch his ass with no regrets.

Lucky for him, my B.O.B. is as quiet as a whisper. A buzzing hum of a whisper, but it won't travel through the wall. Even if it did, he probably wouldn't be home to hear it. If he can keep his live bedmates as quiet, we might make good neighbors after all.

4
Law

RAW TALENT

I've lost count of how many Saturday nights I've spent in dive bars and dance halls named *The Office* or *The Library* over the past five years, but I'm about to add one more. Those names were clever once. Now, they're so common they've become cliché to everyone but the regulars, who see these dark, dusty spaces as community centers.

They know their favorite beer is always on tap and nobody's going to judge them for drinking whiskey from the bottom shelf, but they come for more than the drinks.

On occasion, I've probably been looked at like a regular in a few of these places.

But it's never community I'm looking for when I walk through the doors. I'm in search of raw talent, nothing more.

My new neighbor has an inflated expectation of my last-call exploits. There was a time, but that shit gets old like any other habit.

Tonight, I'm hoping a twenty-one-year-old singer named Derringer Wells actually shows up for his set. Born with a goddamn stage name. Go figure.

Unfortunately, he wasn't born with a whole lot of drive. He's got big dreams, but what little ambition he's got he spends in pursuit of cheap liquor and enthusiastic women. Because he's a typical twenty-one-year-old stuck in a place where there's not much else to do.

What's not typical about him is his polished look, his natural stage presence, and his million-dollar voice. Raw talent wrapped up in the perfect package.

If he'd get his package to the stage a little more often, I could get this kid everything he claims to want.

I know he actually wants it. He just doesn't want to work for it. He's too easily distracted. And far too damn much praise has already been thrown his way. I'm pretty sure he's been told how perfect he is his whole life. And he's definitely bought into his own hype.

He wants to be a star. Definitely wants the money, but he wants the recognition even more. There's nothing wrong with wanting money. That's not the real root of all evil. It's fame that does the dirty work, especially at a young age.

Is it really so fucking hard to just show up? Because that's about all he'd have to do at this point.

The problem is he's already hometown famous, and he hasn't ventured beyond his hometown far enough to know how little that actually means.

He's a big deal here, and here is all he knows.

His family's got oil money. Old oil money. Unlike so many other young men his age from here, he's never had to work a single day in the patch to get a taste of it. His great grandfather was wise with money and ruthless with people.

I'm not sure Derringer inherited either of those qualities. I see an incredibly gifted dumbass. I should move on, let him burn out on his own terms. But I can't yet.

Because I know this kid.

I was him.

Minus the trust fund and the lack of ambition. I had the drive and enough of the talent, but when the first blow knocked me down, I didn't have the strength to get back up again.

Derringer Wells doesn't even have the strength to start, but with everything else he's got, I could guide him through it. If he'd just fucking bother to show up. I check the time on my phone again.

The bartender makes her way down to me. "Looks like the golden boy of Agate Ridge is a no-show tonight."

"Shocking absolutely no one."

"He was here pretty late last night. Drinking and being adored. He got up on stage for a few songs. Even sloppy drunk, he sounded better than anybody else who's ever performed here."

"Of course he did. Speaking of drinking." I slide my empty glass her way.

"He's got a golden voice, Law."

"If only that were enough."

She nods and gives me a weak, sympathetic smile. "People don't usually work too hard for what they don't need, though. And he doesn't really need anything more than what he's already got. If he never becomes a big country music star, he'll still have plenty of money. And he'll always be a popular act around here."

"Yeah, and then one day he'll wake up and realize he's got a stomach full of regret and a coping mechanism that's probably destroying his liver. That's a scary moment. If you're strong enough, it's when you pivot and save yourself. And the one thing Derringer doesn't seem to have is strength."

"He's got a strong voice."

"That's not enough to maintain a career. And unless he pulls his head out of his ass, it's not even going to be enough to start one." I stand from my barstool. "Never mind on the refill. If he shows up, tell him I'm sending him a bill for all my wasted time."

5

Greta

GOING FOR GOLD

The shop that has my car is half an hour away, and the repair cost they just quoted has me wishing I'd taken more than Brick's TV. I was saving for a new car when he proposed last year. Suddenly, a wedding seemed like a better use of the funds.

Maybe not smarter, but more fun. It's all fun and games until you find out your fiancé is a sorry, no-count, lying, sister-in-law-screwing asshole.

The bulk of what I spent was on my dress. It's still hanging in a closet at my mom's house. She's begged me not to make any rash decisions about it. She says just because I'm not marrying Brick doesn't mean I have to let go of my perfect dress.

Magical thinking obviously runs in the family.

"Let me call you back this afternoon," I say to the guy on the phone. "I need to think about it."

"So, you don't want us to fix your car?"

"That's what I need to think about. Just out of curiosity, what would you give me for it as is?"

"Ma'am, we fix cars. We don't buy them."

"But if I decide not to fix it, then what happens?"

"You'll have to come get it."

"It doesn't run."

"I guess you'd have to have it towed then."

"And if I didn't?"

"We'd send you a certified letter asking you to either authorize the repairs or come get the vehicle. If you didn't take any action after thirty days, we'd claim ownership."

"And then you'd sell it, right?"

"Yeah, probably."

"Okay, so let's say all that has already happened. How much would you be able to get for it?"

The young man sighs as if this conversation is draining his life force. "Miss Gaines, please just come get your car."

Why does no one want to give a straight answer to a question anymore? Clear and honest communication has become a lost art, I swear.

"I'll get back to you."

Law's front door closes, but I can't tell if he's coming or going. I heard his shower running last night right after I went to bed. He wasn't out late at all, and I think he came home alone.

His knock on my door makes me jump. I haven't showered yet today. My eyes are probably still swollen from the good, cleansing cry I had over the cereal I ate for lunch. So what if I look sad and unbathed? Who cares?

I'm not trying to impress my neighbor.

I fling the door open and immediately regret the action.

Law looks immaculate in a pair of dark jeans with a crisp, white button-down. His face sports an intentional stubble. His scruffiness is very well maintained. Not to mention his face smells like a woodsy beard oil when he wraps me up in a hug.

Why is he hugging me? Why am I letting him hug me?

Oh, damn. This is a sympathy hug.

It's an I-don't-know-what-else-to-do hug—the hug men give women when they're afraid we might be about to break down.

"You can let go of me now. I'm not going to cry, I promise."

His arms slowly loosen. "You just looked like you could use a hug."

I step out of his arms. "I often look more pathetic than I am. You'll get used to it."

"Nice try." He attempts to make eye contact, but I won't let it happen.

When he realizes I'm not going to be the damsel in distress to his white knight, he says, "Do you need anything?"

"If your drill's not already spoken for this afternoon, I have a TV that needs to be hung on the wall."

"You got it." It takes him no time to get his drill and come back.

"Thanks. Again."

"No worries. When you buy my chips, get the good ones, the kettled cooked ones. And no store brand."

"If I don't figure out how to get my car fixed, I'll have to pay for a ride to the store. You're definitely getting the knock-off chips."

"Hold off on buying them until you have your car back."

"You're still getting the store brand."

"So, what you're saying is you're always cheap."

"Did you miss the part where I told you I was a teacher?"

"This is a nice TV. You obviously splurge on some things."

"It belonged to my ex."

"You took his TV in the divorce? Brutal."

"No divorce. Ex-boyfriend."

"If you stole my TV, I'd break up with you, too."

"After what he did, he would've given me anything I wanted to keep his secret."

"You took the TV and then told everyone his secret, anyway, right?"

"That's exactly what I did. And then he went on a confession tour and told anyone he thought I might've missed. I think his plan was to get out in front of the news and spin it to his advantage. But it's hard to shine a positive light on sleeping with your brother's wife, right? How much do you think I could sell this TV for?"

"Sounds like a great guy. A better revenge would be to keep it and enjoy it."

"I'm not seeking revenge. I need to pay the ransom on my car."

"You don't want to sell your TV for that."

"I hardly even watch it."

"What's wrong with your car?"

"Something about a sensor and some wires. I blacked out for a few seconds after he told me he wanted six-hundred bucks."

"Get the actual names of the parts and let me look up the prices. I can probably put them in for you. Labor is always the biggest part of the bill."

"I'd owe you a whole truckload of chips."

"I don't always work for chips."

Where exactly is he going with this? He better not be about to suggest what I think he's about to suggest.

He shrugs. "How about we trade for it?"

And this is how I go to prison . . .

It's a good thing he's a fast talker. "If you can afford the parts, and I can do the work, how about you let me watch baseball games on your TV?"

"Do you not have one?"

"I do, but it's not this big. And it has a blurry stripe running through the middle of the picture."

"Why don't you just buy yourself a new TV?"

"Because I don't work in the oil field, remember?"

"Right. Why do you keep doing things for me?"

"Because you have things that need to be done. And I can."

"As a driver, you're an asshole. But as a neighbor, you're suspiciously nice."

"You have trust issues. I'm a great driver. And there's no need to be suspicious. I already admitted I have an ulterior motive here."

"Access to my TV."

"For any game I want to watch."

"What if I'm watching something else?"

"You said you hardly watch it."

He's not wrong. It will probably be available for any game he wants to watch on it. I help him lift the TV into place so we can hang it on the bracket he's mounted.

And just like that, where there was once a blank wall, there is now a gargantuan TV.

It's obnoxiously big.

It's ugly, and it ruins the cozy, homey vibe I was going for. But it might be the ticket to getting my car back on the road.

"Fine. You've got a deal."

He extends his hand to shake on it. When my palm slides against his, warmth radiates up my arm. His smile is friendly as we seal our deal with a handshake. No smugness. No smirk to make me wonder if I've just made a mistake.

I suppose even a hermit can let one person take up space on their couch to watch a ballgame now and again. How often is there a baseball game on TV, anyway? It's not such a big deal if he comes around once a week for a few hours. I can still mostly maintain my bubble of isolation.

Anyway, he works nights, so it's not like he'll even be available to watch every game.

"Who's your favorite team?" I ask.

"The Astros. But if they don't make the playoffs and the Rangers do, I gotta support Dallas at that point. After that, I'm for any team that's not the Cardinals."

"Why do you hate the Cardinals?"

"It's a long story."

"They're my favorite bird."

"That's not how you pick a team."

"It might not be how you do it."

"You know nothing about baseball, do you?"

"I know I'm a Cardinals fan."

"It's going to be a short season for you then."

"When does it end?"

"Regular season runs through September. The post-season can go into early November. And then preseason starts again in February."

"There are only a few months out of the year when there aren't baseball games happening?"

"Don't worry. Your team will be out early."

"You don't know that. This could be their year. In fact, I know it is. I can feel it. They're going to take gold at the World Series this year."

"That's not how it . . . you know what? I bet they'll at least get the bronze."

"Oh, they will. You'll see."

6

Law

FLIRTING IN THIS ECONOMY

Greta's reaction when she found out that the cost of the parts to fix her car was only a third of the total estimate the shop had given her will live in my head forever.

She was ready to burn the whole place to the ground.

The only thing that calmed her down was when I assured her that I could definitely do the work and asked, "Can you afford the parts? Because that's all that matters right now."

Once she accepted that, her mood improved considerably. I slipped the youngest mechanic in the garage twenty bucks to help me push her car into the drugstore parking lot next door so their customers wouldn't see me working on it in front of their shop. His boss let it happen, primarily to get Greta out of there, I'm sure. Not that I'm going to tell her that.

"How did you know you could make a side deal like that?" she asks, sitting on the tailgate of my truck with her legs swinging in the breeze while she watches me work on her car.

"It's not a side deal to buy the parts and do the work yourself. You weren't going to pay them to do it, anyway, so it's not like I undercut them to get the job. There was no job in it for them to begin with."

"But I didn't even buy the parts from them. Why weren't they mad that we went to the auto parts store, bought the parts, and then just took my car away?"

"Because they don't need your car taking up space if you're not a paying customer. They're not hurting for business over there."

"Then they should lower their prices. They're robbing people."

"They're not running a charity, Greta. That's just the way it is."

"Well, it sucks."

"That's life."

"It shouldn't have to be, though. What kind of a world do we live in when a teacher can't even afford to get her car fixed?"

"Hey, look. There's a cardinal in that oak tree."

I don't disagree with her, but there's nothing I can do to repair late-stage Capitalism while I'm losing daylight in this parking lot, and I don't want her to get upset again. One, she's a little scary when she gets wound up, but two, it sounds like she's had a rotten run of luck lately.

"I don't see it."

"Huh. I guess it flew away. Maybe it saw me looking at it."

"There was no cardinal, was there? You just wanted me to shut up."

"No, there wasn't a cardinal. But I didn't want you to shut up so much as I just didn't want you to be upset."

"Nothing ever changes until somebody gets upset enough to do something about it."

"Okay. What's your big plan for lowering the cost of car repairs?"

"I hear having a big TV can sometimes get you a discount."

I look up from under her hood to smile at her. "For the record, the TV might not be your only bargaining chip."

"Oh, right. The chips. I forgot about the value of those."

Her smile almost looks a little flirty. I guess we have an inside joke now. That didn't take long. I'm never going to look at a bag of chips again without thinking about her.

"Ow! Fuck!"

"Are you okay?" She hops down from my tailgate in a panic.

"Yeah. Yeah, I'm good. Wrench slipped. That's what I get for not paying attention."

"I distracted you. I'm sorry. Are you sure you're okay?"

"It's just a busted knuckle. I'm fine."

And you can distract me any time.

If I said that out loud, she'd probably lower this hood on my head. And I can't keep an eye on her and attach these wires at the same time, so it's probably safer if I keep my inside thoughts inside.

It takes less than half an hour to swap out the parts. The repair quote really was highway robbery, but I'm not going to bring it up again.

"Moment of truth," I say, motioning for her to get behind the wheel. "Start her up."

Her car hums to life. "You did it!"

"Looks that way. See you at seven."

"What's happening at seven?"

"The Giants are playing the Dodgers."

"I thought your team was the Astros."

"They are my team. But the leagues play each other, so you gotta keep up with everybody."

"There's more than one league?"

"The MLB has two leagues, and each league has three divisions. Did we negotiate game-time snacks?"

"I'll provide chips. If you want anything else, you're on your own."

Oh, I definitely want something else. I already knew I was on my own, though.

Shower sex is undeniably a lot more fun with a partner, but that's life. And until I get upset enough to do something about it, nothing's going to change.

At least I get chips.

If she gets the good ones, I'm going to count it as flirting.

7

Greta

TAKE ME OUT TO THE BALLGAME

Of all the things I never saw myself doing, providing snacks for a man to sit in my living room and watch sports is near the top of the list. I never dated a sports guy, so I never saw this in my future.

I've always had a certain image of men who watch sports on TV. I know a large percentage of the population does it, but my dad doesn't, so I didn't grow up with it. Brick doesn't follow any sports either—although in retrospect, it would've been a far less harmful use of his time.

Asshole.

I had Law categorized as a music guy. I do that, categorize people. Not in a mean way, but there are different types of people, and I assumed he was all about music. If you'd asked me to guess his hobby, I literally would've guessed music. But who wants their job to be their only interest?

It's not like I tutored for fun on the weekends when I was teaching. People aren't that one-dimensional. I know this, yet I've had this rigid system of categorizing them for as long as I can remember.

In my defense, my mom's a realtor, and her hobby is antique fairs and anything to do with home décor. Those things all feel like one category to me. She's into houses and decorating them. She's a house person.

Brick is an architect who spent every moment he could working. Of course, I know now that he wasn't always working. But I believed he was because I had him categorized as a workaholic engineer person. He was just that type.

In reality, I had no idea what type of person he was.

I'm not even sure I know what type of person I am anymore.

But I'm apparently the type who buys overpriced potato chips for her hot and helpful neighbor. He's a music guy. And a sports guy. And he's handy under a hood, so I guess that makes him a car guy, too?

He's still a shitty driver, regardless.

"Knock, knock," he says as he opens my front door. I unlocked it for him ten minutes ago, assuming he would let himself in since I'm expecting him.

I've poured the chips into a bowl. I doubt if he can even tell the difference between these and the store brand if he can't see the bag. He goes straight for them after he puts his beer in the fridge. I bought him beer, too, but I see no reason to admit that since he brought his own.

I watch him crunch the first chip between his teeth. He smiles. "Good choice."

"You got lucky. They were on sale." It's a lie, but I suddenly feel the need to downplay my acquiescence.

"You writing tonight or watching the game with me?"

"I have never seen a baseball game in my life."

"Prepare to get hooked."

"That seems highly unlikely."

"I'll share my chips."

"Your chips?"

"Yeah. You're using them to pay for my labor, remember?"

"That's all you've got to offer to entice me into watching baseball?"

"I'd offer you a beer, but I noticed you already had your own in the fridge. You're still welcome to drink mine if you want to taste a real beer."

"What's wrong with mine?"

"Nothing, if you're in the mood for beer-flavored water."

"What makes yours better?"

"It's from a local micro-brewery, for one thing, so it supports a small business. And it just plain tastes better."

"How does a micro-brewery survive out here?"

"You do know you're not living in a ghost town, right?"

"I know, but are there really that many people here who drink beer?"

"Yes. Get yourself one, and you'll understand why."

I had planned to listen to a podcast in my room while he watched his game, but now I'm intrigued about this local beer.

"You're more high maintenance than my first impression led me to believe. Fancy chips. Pretentious beer. What else am I going to find out about you, neighbor?"

"I'm an open book. What do you want to know?"

"Have you ever discovered a big star?"

"A few who might be someday. And one who could absolutely be a big star if he didn't have such a big ego."

"Isn't that a normal part of being a star?"

"It's one thing when the ego develops along the way. It's a lot harder to get there when you arrive on the scene with an ego that enters the room five paces before you."

"Oh. It's not the size of his ego; it's that he hasn't earned it."

"Exactly. Here comes the first pitch."

I sit next to him on my couch and promise myself I won't ask too many questions during the game. And also, that I won't fall asleep, which might require me to ask a few questions.

8

Lau

A PERFECTLY IMPERFECT GAME

She keeps apologizing every time she asks a question, but I love that she's asking. At first, I thought she might be faking her curiosity, but after a few interruptions, her sincerity couldn't be doubted.

Greta doesn't just want to know the reason for the calls; she has solutions for how the game could be better.

In a sports bar, or even in a living room full of baseball fans trying to watch a game, she would be the most annoying person in the crowd. But here, in her own space with her head tilted and the wheels so obviously spinning in her head as she listens to my answers, she's fascinating.

She's solving problems baseball never knew it had.

"Did your ex-boyfriend not watch baseball?"

"No. He was too busy watching his pencil dick slide in and out of his brother's wife."

I do a spit-take with my beer. That escalated quickly. I didn't expect her to revisit that detail, and it's definitely not what I want her to be thinking about right now.

"Any chance you're getting hungry for something more substantial than chips?" I ask.

"I am not cooking you dinner."

"Actually, I was offering to have something delivered."

"Oh, fun. Like going to the concession stand."

"Yeah, just like that." I open the food delivery app on my phone. "Do you like Indian food?"

"That doesn't seem like baseball food."

"Well, I don't know anywhere that delivers hotdogs, so how spicy do like your curry?"

"Medium. I can't believe there's Indian food here."

"Don't get too excited. You haven't had it yet. It might not live up to your standards."

"I'm honestly not that picky."

"That explains your ex."

She laughs, which was my intention, but it was a risky comment. If I'd thought about it before the words flew out of my mouth, I might not have said it. If she'd defended him, I'd be enjoying the rest of this game a whole lot less.

Then she says, "Brick in no way brought enough spice to the table to be compared to Indian food."

That clears things up well enough.

"Ouch. I hope there aren't any women out there who'd say that about me."

"I could say a lot worse about him, but I don't want to ruin a perfectly good baseball game."

"I appreciate that. But you can feel free to vent whenever you need to. It can help, sometimes."

The score is fourteen to four in the bottom of the fourth. This isn't anywhere near a perfect ballgame. And listening to her trash her ex is never going to ruin anything for me.

"Are you blind!" she suddenly yells at the TV. "In what world was that a strike?"

She catches on quick. But that was a strike by a mile.

Greta needs to yell, and baseball offers plenty of options to take your frustrations out on a stranger in the privacy of your own living room. No consequences, just cleansing.

When the day comes that she stops yelling, I'll know she's gotten the worst of her heartbreak out of her system. Until then, she can tell me all about how unfair the world is, and I'll listen to her reinvent baseball during every game she'll watch with me.

She takes my mind off things that bother me a hell of a lot more. It's a fair trade.

9

Greta

Same Old Song

Law doesn't work every night, but he's out tonight. The realization that I feel uneasy when he's not on the other side of the wall pisses me off. Sure, I moved here to be a hermit, but also to remember that I'm a strong, capable woman who doesn't need a man in her life.

But here I am, wishing my neighbor was home so I'd feel safer.

I should probably get out more myself. It's been nearly a month, and I still haven't ventured too far off the path from the duplex to the grocery store or the gas station. I've got the hermit part down.

It's time to exert my independence before I lose it entirely.

Where would I even go? What would I do?

There is a pretty well-known cavern not far from here. They offer guided tours. I'd be around other people without the obligation to engage with them in any way.

I could go shopping—or looking, according to my bank balance. There are antique stores in town, and Mom would love pictures of all the great finds she's missing out on. Plus, it would make her feel better to see proof that I'm not hiding away from the world.

Staying inside and alone as much as I have been isn't healthy.

And thinking about my neighbor so often is becoming a problem. I'd almost stopped seeing spontaneous images of him in my mind, and then I saw him in real life sitting on his back patio, drinking his morning coffee in nothing but a pair of black boxer briefs while I was hanging my laundry on a line like a pilgrim because my damn dryer is broken and our landlord isn't exactly on the ball when it comes to repairs, and let's just say when I envision him now, I'm more confident in my dimensions.

This should make me not want to see him face-to-face ever again, but it's impressive what the mind can put aside until it's safe to access the information.

I actually look forward to the next baseball game, which is tomorrow at four. Astros at the Cardinals. Our favorite teams kick off a three-game series in St. Louis. And his Astros are going down.

If only he was...

Okay, that's it. I've got to get out of here tomorrow morning and go where the people are. Soak up some sun. See some birds. Put some space between me and Law.

We are friends, and that's it.

He's attractive and funny and kind . . . but I've already overshared about my pathetic life. And that's a line you can't uncross. He's never going to see me as anything other than his quirky neighbor, an emotionally damaged woman who has no filter and will probably never truly understand all the rules of baseball, despite his valiant efforts.

Not to mention, if he knew what I'm actually writing in here, he'd laugh his head off. Or avoid me at all costs. That would be worse.

I'd be devastated if he ever thought ours was only a friendship of convenience, that I was trying to use him in any way. Our budding friendship actually means something to me. I'm still not sure how this happened. It's like he barged in and became my friend when I wasn't looking.

He won't take no for an answer once he decides to help with something. He's kind of a space invader. He might have a touch of white knight syndrome, which I hate. He occasionally toes the line on mansplaining.

But he's just so damn likeable.

Law is more comfortable to be around than anyone I've ever known. Unfortunately, he's far too easy to insert into my fantasies, too. It's not my fault he fits so nicely into them.

I guarantee I'm not the only woman who thinks of him that way. There are probably women in every bar within a fifty-mile radius who are hoping to run into him every time they show up.

He always comes home alone, though.

It doesn't make sense. Not that I'm wishing for him to bring home another woman. On second thought, maybe I do want that. If I knew he was seeing other women, it might make things easier.

The more time that passes with him sleeping alone on his side of the wall and me all alone in my bed over here... well, the more implausible scenarios my brain generates.

Two months ago, I was engaged. Law was a complete stranger to me then, and now, he stars in all my fantasies. Not a faceless stranger, but him.

Unmistakably him.

The advice to get under a new man to get over an old one exists for a reason. I know my fantasies are normal, especially given what I was going through when we met. I'm not afraid of my sexuality. It's the non-sexual fantasies that scare the shit out of me.

I see him in situations that will never happen, like the two of us exploring a new city, watching baseball in a different living room, waking up together, sharing dinner in a real dining room in a big renovated farmhouse with leaded transoms over the doors and rocking chairs on the front porch...

I've created a whole future fantasy life with him.

This is beyond unhealthy. I'm losing it. Definitely setting myself up for another round of heartbreak when I have to leave here. This was not the plan.

I will eventually have to face reality again. And the reality is, I'm going to have to go back to teaching. Or to some other real job. I tear out the notebook page I've been scribbling on, ball it up, and toss it at the small trashcan next to my bed.

It hits the rim, bounces off, and lands in a pile with my other discarded, crumpled pages from tonight's writing session.

Maybe I should try writing on my laptop again. Somewhere along the way, I convinced myself that writing by hand would result in more authentic words. Using a pen isn't working any better than the keyboard.

Not every page gets torn out and thrown away. I have pages and pages of unfinished projects that I've kept. Finishing something would feel like such a win right now. Even when I get off to a good start, I hit a road block.

Inspiration still strikes and words still come to me, but they always stop too soon.

They say the hardest part of writing is getting started, but that's not true for me. The hardest part is knowing what comes next. I'm great at beginnings, but that's as far as I get.

I have one finished piece. One.

You can't be a successful songwriter with just one song. Besides, even if a miracle happened, and that song did become a success, it's nobody's dream to be a one-hit wonder.

10

Law

A Shot and a Half

I wake to the sound of my overnight guest dropping a glass in the kitchen.

And if the sound of glass shattering on a tile floor isn't loud enough, the volume on the expletive that follows could wake the dead. There's no doubt it will wake Greta.

Perfect. Not regretting last night's decision at all.

My eyes are still struggling to focus as I open my bedroom door and stagger toward the kitchen, hoping I don't have to put my shoes on and drive this bumbling idiot to the emergency room.

"Mornin'," Derringer says. "Sorry about the glass."

"I'm more worried about my neighbor, who I'm sure was still asleep until you yelled at this unholy hour on a Sunday morning."

His disheveled morning look would make for a great publicity photo. All he'd have to do is spread that white-toothed grin across his face and he'd go viral. Young women would flock to his comments to tell him how pretty he is—and a host of other stuff they really shouldn't post to the eternal archive of the internet.

I look down at his bare feet to be sure there's no blood soaking into my grout.

If that sounds uncaring, it's because I don't care.

Any potential cuts on Derringer's feet mean far less to me than the thought of Greta losing sleep.

His toes are all still intact. Charmed as always.

"Don't move. Let me sweep this shit up."

"It's not like I did it on purpose. I needed water."

"I have no doubt. You probably also need food."

"That sounds like a terrible idea."

"You burned through your quota of terrible ideas last night."

"Oh, come on. It couldn't have been that bad."

"If you were already signed, PR would be stirring anti-anxiety meds into their coffee this morning. Do everyone, including yourself, a goddamn favor and stay off stages you haven't been invited to perform on."

"I hop up on stage spontaneously all the time. The fans love it."

"Yeah, well, you can't spontaneously take your pants off in public."

"To be fair, I'm pretty sure the fans loved that, too."

"For your own safety, please get out of my kitchen." I sweep a path for him. "You came close to having your *fans* seeing you get arrested."

"I wouldn't have been the first musician to get arrested. Besides, any publicity is good publicity, right?"

He laughs as he walks away. The urge to whack him in the back of the head with the broom handle is strong. But I resist because he's done enough damage to his body on his own in the past eight hours.

"No. It's not all good. There's a difference between an intentional stage dive, and drunkenly falling off the stage."

"Well, I was intentionally drunk, so give me credit for that much at least."

"Whatever is eating at you and making you so damn self-destructive, you need to get a handle on it now before it's too late. Take my word for it."

"Is this the moment where you share a cautionary tale about some singer nobody's ever heard of, who could've had it all if he hadn't blown his big chance? Spare me."

"Those stories may be a dime a dozen, but they're real. And they're all the same."

"Yeah, but I'm different. Because I can actually fucking sing."

"They could all fucking sing! That's the tragedy. You're better than most. But you're not smarter. Having the voice is the bare minimum you need to get half a shot."

"Well, I've got three times the voice of anybody else. So, I guess that gives me a shot and a half."

"Glad to know you can still do math when you're hungover."

"I'm not hungover."

"You will be in a few hours. And if you puke on my carpet, I'll rip your golden vocal cords out with my bare hands."

"Where are my keys?"

"Probably in your pocket. But your truck's sitting in an impound lot."

"What? How the fuck did that happen?"

"Go back to sleep, Derringer. I'll explain it all when you're sober."

"Can I get that glass of water now?"

I white-knuckle the broom handle. This kid has no idea how lucky he got last night. "Sit down. I'll bring it to you. I can't afford to replace all my glasses every time you get thirsty."

"If you'd just get me a deal already, you could afford all the glasses you want."

"Right. You've got the whole industry all figured out."

"I'm just saying... whenever you're ready, me and my golden vocal cords will make you a rich man."

He's nearly asleep by the time I bring him his water. I toss half of it in his face.

Wouldn't want my cash cow to get dehydrated.

He flips me off, downs the rest of the water, and passes out on my couch again.

I'm going to have to take more than beer over to Greta's for the game later. Maybe some flowers.

And ear plugs, just in case I decide to babysit the golden boy again.

I want to believe I won't rescue him twice, but even as I watch him with his mouth hanging open, sleeping off last night's drunken antics on my couch, I know I'd do it again. His dad can (and will) buy his way out of any trouble he gets into, but that won't save him from himself.

Money can't buy what Derringer Wells needs most. And it's damn sure not a recording contract. He needs a swift kick in the ass. On a regular basis.

11

Greta

Musty Memories

Even as I snap my last photo before we exit the cavern, I know I'm never going to use these pictures for anything. It's a type of beauty that the camera on my phone can't capture, anyway. But we all photographed every new section we entered like the predictable tourists we were.

I've deleted so many pictures from my phone over the last few months. At least the cavern shots will never be painful.

I pull out of the parking lot and head downtown. I've promised myself I'll stay out and about for at least three hours today. Baby steps.

The first inhale as I push through the door of a dusty, musty antique shop transports me straight back to my childhood. Mom dragged me to so many small-town shopping districts, and in and out of every antique store that was open.

I have some fun memories of going to the big antique fairs with her, but those were mostly outdoors, and the smells I remember are the kettle corn and the strawberry lemonade she'd buy to keep me happily tagging along from booth to booth.

But the indoor shops? They all had this exact smell. I hated it back then, and to be honest, it still stinks, but I loved the shops because in those, Mom bribed me with whatever silly trinkets I fell in love with. They were my own antiques.

She'd have her find-of-the-day, and I'd have mine. Whether I was getting a new giant pencil or piece of old, but cheap, costume jewelry, I was happy because I'd found it for myself.

No matter how hard Mom tried, I never developed her love of real antiques. The mall won out. I wanted things that were new. But sometimes now, something with a little history to it catches my eye.

I snap a picture of an old cash register and send it to her. There is one just like it on the buffet in her dining room. As a little girl, I'd give everyone at the table a handwritten bill and then ring them up on that cash register after dinner.

My family would all play along with my pretend restaurant, but my favorite aunt would give me a dollar every time. She'd say, "A woman should always be able to pay for her own meal. Promise me you'll never be so dependent on a man that you can't take yourself out to dinner."

I had no idea what she meant, but I was always happy to get the dollar. Once I was old enough to understand the message, I was happy for the advice, too.

At least I wasn't financially dependent on Brick. I may never be wealthy, but my life won't be a lie.

Traipsing through these shops is not how I want to spend all my Saturdays, but I'm content with antiquing this afternoon.

Mom responds to my message. She loves the cash register, but she wants to know if I've checked out the schools here yet. She's more worried about the fact that I quit my job than my canceled wedding.

I've tried to explain this isn't a permanent move, but she's never going to believe that I can actually afford to take a little time off. I have to live frugally while I'm here, but I can do that.

There is nothing I want to buy right now, anyway. Shopping doesn't cheer me up the way it does her. It's only fun for me if I'm already happy. I will be again someday.

Today, I'm just looking. Just browsing to keep my mind off other things.

I'm not as sad and angry as I was when I arrived in Agate Ridge. I'm just sort of here, walking around in a semi-emotionless haze every day.

But not all day.

I can laugh again. And I catch myself smiling at least once every day. It's progress that I mostly owe to Law, but I'm not hanging my happiness on him.

I'm my own happy little hermit. Almost.

12

Law

RAISING THE STAKES

I decided against flowers because I remembered Greta had a bowl full of individually wrapped chocolates on her kitchen counter when I came over to hang her TV. It was nearly empty the last time I was at her place.

"Knock, knock. I hope you're not on some weird sugar detox." I hold up the bag.

"You're refilling my bowl?"

"Unless I got the wrong ones."

"You got it right. Thanks." She opens the chocolate and dumps it into the bowl. One gets stuck in the bag, and she tosses it to me after she shakes it out.

"I have to unwrap it myself?"

"You want me to feed it to you, too?"

"I mean, if you're offering."

"I'm not." She takes a chocolate for herself. "I probably should be detoxing from these things, but they're my gold stars."

"You use them as a reward system?"

"Yeah. It's motivating to know you get a reward when you complete a task."

"If you're in kindergarten."

"There is no age limit for task completion rewards." She sticks her tongue out at me, and then she pops the candy into her mouth. "I got you something, too."

"You better have. If you didn't get my chips, you're going to have to finish paying me off with your own menial labor."

"Like what, doing your laundry?"

"For starters."

"I got your chips, but I am never doing your laundry." She opens her fridge and pulls out a six-pack. "And I got you real beer. You're welcome."

"You got that beer because you like it better than the stuff you used to buy. Admit it."

"I admit nothing."

She unwraps another chocolate.

"What task are you rewarding yourself for now?"

"Remembering to buy the chips."

"Do you get a reward for getting out of bed in the morning?"

"Some days I do."

"Was today one of those days?"

"It started out a little rough. What did you break that made you yell like that so early in the morning?"

"I didn't break anything. The area's hottest up-and-coming country singer broke a glass, and the outburst that woke you up was his."

"Ah, a singer. No wonder he has such strong lungs."

"That's about all he's got going for him."

"How old is he?"

"Twenty-one."

"Were you so wise and responsible at twenty-one?"

"No, which is exactly why I know how badly he's about to fuck up."

"Well, if you're going to fuck up, your early twenties is the time to do it."

"Some of us fuck up worse than others." I open both the beers she's set on the coffee table. The caps twist off, but she always waits for me to open them. I know she could open her own, but it's become part of our routine for me to do it. And I like it.

"I bet you weren't so bad," she says.

"You'd lose that bet. I bet you never fucked up on any level."

"And you'd lose that bet."

We clink the necks of our bottles together and settle back against her couch cushions to watch the ballgame. My 'Stros are going to blow her Cards out of the water.

"Speaking of bets, care to wager on the game?" I ask.

"Hmm, what'd you have in mind?"

"If the Astros win this game by more than five, you have to cook me dinner tonight. If not, I'll cook."

"Why such low stakes? Not showing much faith in your team there. If the Astros are up on my Cardinals by more than five runs at any point in this game, I'll not only cook you dinner, I'll serve it to you naked."

"Whoa. That's a lot of confidence in a team you weren't even a fan of until a few weeks ago. Playing a sport you'd never watched. You sure you want to risk that much?"

"Go big or go home."

She extends her hand, and I shake on the bet. But I never want her to go back home. Not that Agate Ridge is home for me, either. I'm not sure where home is for me, anymore.

13

Greta

How I'm Not Gonna Die

I still can't believe the Cardinals failed me like this. But if there's one thing I'm good at, it's doubling down when I should've cut my losses. I raised the stakes, and now, I'm his naked beer maid while we wait on the grocery store take-and-bake pizza in my oven to finish cooking.

Honestly, I think he expected me to try to get out of it, but I don't skip out on a bet. Besides, I hate being underestimated.

So, I took it all off like the supremely confident woman I'm currently pretending to be as his eyes roam over my body.

Law accepts the cold bottle from my hand and snakes his other arm around my lower back to pull me closer as he takes the first sip of the beer.

"How do you like it?" I know it's his favorite beer, but I'm playing a role here, and staying in character is my only hope of getting through this.

"It seems a little more hoppy than usual." He touches the tip of the bottle between my breasts, and I try not to jump. When he pulls it down between my ribs, I maintain eye contact. He drags it lower, pausing at my belly button for a moment, trying to read my reaction, but I'm doing everything in my power not to give him one.

My gaze is steely. It has to be. The brown bottle slides down my abdomen. A shiver wracks my spine when he slips it between my legs.

Am I really about to let him do what I think he's about to do?

The glass lip is no longer cold when it makes contact with my pussy. He continues his critique. "I think it needs a little sweetness to take the edge off."

Okay, I did not expect this when I decided to pay up, but I'm not going to let him unnerve me. I can match his energy.

He glides the mouth of the bottle back and forth between my seam. I smile, still staring straight into his eyes even as my walls clench in anticipation. When he pushes it inside me, he almost breaks my resolve. He doesn't go far, just the first few inches, but my heels leave the ground, and my breath stutters.

I forget to breathe at all when he brings the bottle back to his mouth and traces the rim with the tip of his tongue before taking his second sip. "Yeah, that's better."

There's a wicked glint in his eyes. A challenge.

Two can play, music man.

I close my fingers over his wrapped around the bottle and pull it in my direction. Leaning my head down, but making sure my eyes stay lifted to his, I let my tongue trace the rim. His attempt to mask his body's reaction falls short.

Having him off his game could be fun. No way am I stopping now.

Again, I trace the mouth of the bottle . . . and then, I dip my tongue inside, curling it as I pull it back out. His jaw locks, and his eyes hood. I may have lost the bet, but I'm going to wipe that smug smile right off his gorgeous face.

I inch the bottle into my mouth and close my lips around it, and then I pull it out—oh, so slowly, suctioning my cheeks before I release it. I tongue the opening again, reaching deeper this time.

His eyes are glued to the show. Turning the tables on him is so much fun.

I slip my tongue farther into the bottle and twist it slightly.

He lets out a prolonged groan.

I pump my mouth on the bottle a few times, letting my tongue go deeper.

My confidence soars . . .

Right up to the moment I realize how badly I've fucked up.

Oh, shit. The stakes just got too damn high.

Increasing the force when I pull only makes it worse. I've created a vacuum.

My tongue is stuck in this fucking bottle.

Panic rises, and I'd rather die than have him know what's happening, but if I don't let him know what's happening, I may literally die with my tongue stuck in this fucking bottle!

This cannot be how I die.

Law's confused expression makes it clear he's not entirely sure what's happening.

I point to the bottle. "Izz sthuck!"

His mouth quirks, and I swear, if he laughs right now, I'll slam this bottle into the wall and stab him with a broken shard.

"Okay, I need you to try to calm down," he says, making the condescending lowering motion with his hands.

What you need is to gird your loins and hope I don't hit an artery when I stab you with a piece of broken glass!

Forcing the tip of his pinky between my tongue and the lip of the bottle, he manages to press his knuckle against my tongue, and then tip the bottle just enough to break the vacuum.

He quickly slips the bottle off my swollen tongue. His smile is heroic.

And then he laughs.

And, so do I.

I laugh hysterically.

I'm not sure if it's the sheer relief of knowing I'm not going to die, or just the absolute absurdity of the whole situation. Of all the fantasies I've had about being naked with him, never once was there a bottle hanging off my tongue.

He wraps both his arms around me, and my laughter subsides as his mouth closes on mine. I've forgotten all about being naked until his warm hand slides down my back to cup my ass. I don't need to be someone else anymore.

Breaking the kiss, he murmurs, "Can I get another taste if I promise to leave the bottle on the table?"

"The answer is yes," I confess. "With or without the bottle. Your call."

"No bottle this time," he says, but he picks it up, anyway. "Let's take it to the bedroom with us in case we want to use it again later."

"Later? Somebody's confident."

"Trust me, we're going to be a while."

"Not if we never get started."

"Oh, we're about to get something started, sweetheart."

14

Greta

RAW HONESTY

Lying on my bed with my legs spread while Law lowers his face between them, I have to rally my confidence again. The vulnerability of intimacy dawns with inopportune clarity.

I'm not afraid this man is going to hurt me in any way, but still, being on this threshold has me suddenly apprehensive. Officially crossing the line from neighbors to lovers... I don't want to stop it, but the stakes between us will always be higher after this.

He doesn't plant soft kisses and work up to more.

Just like he doesn't knock on my door, he charges right into my body, too. And Jesus fuck, does he know how to make an entrance. His hot mouth is definitely welcome.

The back of my head sinks deeper into the pillow as his tongue probes me while the rest of his mouth massages tender places in a way that fingers and devices will never be able to replicate.

If this is what it means to be taken to church, then hallelujah! Your girl's found religion.

I grasp at the sheets while he teases around my clit. When his tongue slows, flattening to blanket my nerve endings with heightening heat and an obscenely sublime increase in pressure, my hips wantonly rock upward, seeking more.

His mouth takes the cue, closing in to suck my clit for a moment before going back to the tongue lashing and mouth grinding actions that make my head loll from side-to-side. He alternates now, giving my clit more friction each time he returns to it.

The scruff on his jaw lightly abrades my skin like the gentle scratch of sharp fingernails, teetering on the edge of a near-tickling scrape, a sensation that I desperately need to either intensify or stop altogether because it's pulling me into a frenzied purgatory. The maddening agitation, contrasting with the strengthening smooth, slick caresses of his tongue, ignites a simultaneous burst of sparklers behind my eyelids and in my core. Quick bright flashes sync with the tingling surges of heat rushing from my core, pulsing into my legs, making them quiver before the muscles seize and attempt to squeeze my thighs shut.

His shoulders tense to hold my legs open until I buck and pant my way through the most intense orgasm I've had in ages. Possibly ever.

We have obliterated the line between friends and lovers. There is no crossing back over once you've flooded his face.

This isn't a drunken, fumbling quickie that we can both ignore afterwards or decide to laugh off and promise ourselves will never happen again. We are too sober to make excuses, and this is too vividly intentional to ignore.

And we're just getting started.

He hungrily kisses his way up my body, stopping to lavish my nipples with the same attention he gave my clit. I look down, and the sight of his face at my breast spawns a lusty haze that clouds my vision. It feels far more sensual than I was prepared for.

I can't deny there's a connection between us that transcends the physical, but I didn't expect to feel this level of comfort with him.

His mouth reaches my neck, and he bites playfully at the soft spot above my collar bone, sending a spasm of pleasure across my shoulders. It spreads down my chest, and my nipples perk up again as the phantom sensation of his hot mouth surrounds them.

My pussy hasn't forgotten the mastery of his mouth either. He left it soaked and clenched, but I feel another round of my juices gush with his body hovering over mine.

"You are so goddamn beautiful, Greta." His kiss shuts out the world like brocade Victorian bed curtains have been drawn around us. Everywhere else is dark and far away.

The crown of his heavy cock lurches at my entrance. He's thick and hard, and despite my abundant wetness, the increasing pressure of the stretch as he inches inside me causes the slightest, most delectable pain. I know it will subside once he's all the way in, but I almost don't want it to go away.

I think he's only starting slow because he knows it's been a while since I've taken a dick. He doesn't need to. I assume he'll abandon the gentleness soon, but he could fuck me like a savage right out of the gate.

I'm dying for him to use me, to take what he needs . . . to confirm he doesn't see me as too meek or too fragile to handle him.

Hearing him call me beautiful was affirming and nice, but I don't need nice right now. I need raw and dirty and rough. I need to know he sees me as a woman for all occasions—one he respects, but knows he can fuck like he doesn't.

And the only way that works is if the respect is genuine and complete.

I don't want false respect that has limitations ever again. I want a man selfless enough to risk losing me with honesty, not another coward who "protects" me with lies. I'll never pretend again. If it's not real, I don't want it.

"Stop treating me like I'm breakable."

"I thought maybe we should take our time."

"Not tonight, Law. No restraints. I want to know who you are, not who you think I want you to be."

"You promise not to hide anything from me either?"

"I'll unleash my inner whore completely." I smile because I can't resist deflecting just a little with teasing flirtation. That's the real me, though. It's honest.

"Mmmm, I can't wait to meet her."

"Then stop stalling already."

His eyes narrow, and I think we're about to get real honest with each other.

15

Law

Man Cannot Live on Pizza Alone

Panting on my back with Greta's head on my chest is not where I saw this night going. To be clear, I'm not complaining, but my head's been spinning since she took her clothes off.

The moment she raised the stakes on our bet, I was sure she'd never pay up if she lost. I fully intended to give her a hard time about it, too—already had some good zingers queued up.

Thought maybe I might even get to see her blush while she tried to weasel her way out of following through.

Yeah, remind me not to underestimate her again.

She didn't hesitate for a moment, just took her clothes off like I'd already seen her naked a million times before.

Hell, I may have blushed, but she sure didn't.

And when she pulled my beer bottle to her mouth . . . let's just say if I get dementia and only a single memory survives, it will be that one.

Actually, I'll probably remember her tongue getting stuck, too.

I don't mean to laugh in this tender moment, but damn, what a hilarious precursor to such amazing sex.

"What's so funny?"

"What would your first guess be?"

She sighs, and it's fucking adorable because I know she knows exactly what I'm laughing about. "My tongue getting stuck in that bottle?"

"Come on. Even you have to see the humor in it at this point."

"What I lack in seduction skills, I make up for with comedy."

"You do not lack in seduction skills, sweetheart." I tickle her shoulder just to feel her squirm against me. "It was funny, but the moments before your tongue got stuck are a hell of a lot more memorable."

"I wish I could scrub the whole episode from my brain."

"Don't say that. I don't want you to wish away any moments we spend together. And if you forgot that part, you might forget everything that came after."

"No, trust me, I won't ever forget what came after. Or after that. Or after that."

"If you keep flattering me, there might be more to come."

"I can't take any more. It's a good thing I don't have to go anywhere in the morning. I'm not sure I'll be able to walk."

"What did I just tell you about flattering me?"

We both laugh, and I like the way it sounds. Our laughter occurs together a lot. And I hope what happened in her bedroom this evening happens a lot from now on.

"Hey, what happened to that pizza you put in the oven?"

She bolts upright. "Oh, shit! I forgot all about the pizza."

Her nose crinkles as she sniffs the air. "Wait a minute. It should be burned to a crisp by now, but I don't smell anything. Do you?"

"No. Are you sure you turned the oven on?"

Hanging her head, she admits, "I was so nervous about being naked in front of you that I nearly forgot to take the plastic off the pizza. Then I was so overcome with relief that my brain had kicked in before I let it melt all over . . . everything that happened right after is a blur. I have no memory of turning on the oven. And since the smoke detectors haven't gone off, I think it's safe to assume I didn't."

"We would've been too busy to take it out if you had, and now I'm twice as hungry, so it'll taste even better. Some mistakes work out for the best."

She smiles, but there's no laughter. I can't decode the look in her eyes, but I'd sell my soul to keep it from being regret.

Please don't let her regret this.

I watch her shimmy into a pair of shorts without bothering with underwear. If she knew how hot I find that . . . never mind, she definitely knows. Her boobs shake a little as she pulls a t-shirt over her head. She never goes braless. I like this post-sex, free-the-nipple version of her. Suddenly, my stomach growls like an angry bear.

It's not the first time since I moved here that I've found myself more interested in pizza than pussy. But with Greta, I am definitely still interested in the latter. I prefer to think of this pizza as a precursor to round two.

Or round three, as the case may be. It's not bragging if it's true.

16

Greta

People Do What They Do

I know it's not unusual for the sex to be exceedingly hot in the beginning, and of course, someone can easily consume your thoughts when you're at that stage, but damn.

Walking past the take-and-bake pizza in the grocery store should not make my panties wet. And I should not feel the urge to take my clothes off when an errant dog toy shaped like a baseball bounces off my foot on the sidewalk.

I roll the ball back to the clumsy black dog who's anxiously scampering between all the cars searching for it. Poor guy. His owner runs over to thank me with an empty leash in her hand.

"That ball is his favorite thing in the world. When it fell out of his mouth and started rolling down the sidewalk, he snapped the leash ring right off his collar! Time for a harness, I guess."

"We've all got our favorite things." I shrug and give her a smile.

"Thanks again," she says, jogging off to catch up with her dog, who is already running in circles in the park across the street.

The smell of strong coffee and fresh lemon pound cake hypnotizes me when I walk into Coffee & Cake. In their defense, all the clever coffee shop and bakery names were probably already taken. It's kind of refreshing to be told exactly what to expect. No puns, no mystery. They've got coffee, and they've got cake.

What they don't have is Law right next door, exuding his sex vibes through the wall. Okay, truthfully, he's probably still sleeping, but I know he's over there, and that's enough to prevent me from getting any writing done.

I need to be here, sitting at my favorite little corner table, half-hidden by a giant plastic monstera plant in need of a good dusting. This is where my creativity flows best—with a steamy cup of dark roast and a slice of whatever looks the most decadent.

The coffee is hot and the red velvet cake is fluffy and light, but just dense enough to support a thick layer of cream cheese frosting. I lick my fork.

And all of a sudden, Law's right back on center stage in my head.

I can't write about him. Or us. All the best country or Americana songs about relationships are about the painful end or the mess in the middle, not the thrill at the beginning.

If that's even what we're doing. We haven't put a label on it. We just keep doing it.

And doing it. And...

Even if I could sell a song about a new relationship, I've already written one of those. My catalogue needs to be diversified.

I didn't write my only finished song about Brick. He and I were already long past all the initial attraction stuff. I think I wrote it about what I was longing for, the life I wished I was living.

The life I'm living now comes a lot closer to those lyrics.

What if that's my problem? Maybe I can't write when I'm happy. I've never bought into the genius of the emotionally tormented artist, but it was a lot easier to write a happy song when I was unhappy than it is to write a sad one now.

I guess I could try to create a smoldering, sexy song without obsessing about the emotions. Could that work on its own? Does anybody even want that?

It seems like every other new hit is an upbeat let's-go-to-the-club-and-do-shotties-with-the-hotties pop-country chart climber. Nothing wrong with those, but it's not something I'll probably ever write. I used to love some of those songs back when I was going out with the girls a lot.

Then, along came Brick, and I lost the desire for those kinds of nights, and those kinds of songs lost their appeal.

At this point in my life, I'd rather write about a dog breaking his leash to chase a ball. I should've gotten his name.

I drag the tines of my fork through the frosting on my cake, making a heart and then a question mark. As I watch the lines form, I think of my fingernails running down Law's back, his scruffy jaw marking my inner thighs and my neck...

Now, that's the stuff that belongs in a song.
It's not enough, though. Not even for a song.
Sex is never enough. It's usually the first thing to fade.
Then again, for some people, it's the only good thing that stays. In those toxic relationships that have a chokehold on some couples. That crazy love that isn't love at all. I have a friend who spent years in a broken relationship like that.

Maybe I should be glad the sex faded between Brick and me; not that it was ever that great to begin with, now that I look back on it. Now that I have something so much better to compare it to. Hell, I had better before him, too. Maybe that's why it was easier to let go of whatever we had left. So many maybes.

We weren't great together. But we stuck around long enough to get comfortable. We put in the time and knew all the mundane stuff, like which allergy medicine the other preferred and the name of the coworker they couldn't stand.

Would've been helpful if I'd known I was the only one whose sex life had gone stale.

I should've never judged my friend for staying when she just had a different type of comfort. Maybe our own lived experiences are all we can ever truly understand.

But why do people put themselves through hell when there's nothing beyond the physical? What is it that draws people back into those black holes of heartbreak just for another round of hot sex?

Am I that boring? Or are they just addicted to the darkness of an obsessive attraction?

Without another thought, I pick up my pen.

The Way I Love the Dark

It's a stunner of a sunrise
The promise of a clean start
Birds singin' in the trees
As a clear dawn breaks

Know it's a light that should fill my heart
But the way I love the dark

New boots for an old rundown bar
The promise of a heartbreak
Sunglasses on my dash
Parked next to your truck

Yeah, I know I should avoid this place
But it's fun here in the dark.

Last call always comes way too soon
The promise of more regret
Fumbled keys in the lock
Fallin' on your bed

No denying this is a mistake
But it feels right in the dark

Drag my fingernails down your back
The promise of one more lie
Empty words from your mouth

Tangled up in these sheets

It's still impossible to forget
The way you love me in the dark

I'll stall when my friends ask me why
The promise of all their wrath
Too shameful to explain
Sure I'll do it again

I wish I understood it myself
Just the way I love the dark

It's something. It's more words than I've been able to string together since I wrote the song about longing. But I don't long for what's happening in these lyrics. I may have been a fool for far too long, but when the end finally came, I could let go.

I wouldn't spend another night with Brick if he crawled across broken glass and begged.

I've just written about a woman who knows she's hurting herself when she has the power to stop it. Or she should have the power. But what does it mean? Is it about reconciling her loss of control, or maybe facing the fact that she never had as much as she thought she did?

Huh. I close my notebook and slip it back into my purse.

Writing is so weird. Just when you're afraid your creative well has run completely dry, new words show up out of nowhere.

17

Law

WHEN RESTRAINT FAILS

This is the third gig in a row where Derringer has actually shown up. On time and sober enough to perform. I can't help but wonder if there's a new someone in his life who's a good influence on him, but his eyes aren't stopping on anyone in particular in the crowd, and I don't see a smitten young woman on a barstool, staring at him with hearts in her eyes.

I'm afraid to let myself believe he might be straightening up for his own good. Few twenty-one-year-olds do, but miracles happen, I guess.

I stay until he's safely off the stage with a local beauty hanging on him at the bar, but I leave him with some parting words of wisdom.

"If you plan on getting stupid tonight, please do it away from here. You sounded good up there. Don't follow a good performance with a bad decision."

"I won't. I'm just going to have a few drinks and then head home." He smiles with a quick sideways glance at the young woman attached to his side, as if I might not have understood why he'd be wanting to head home soon.

"Be safe. See you next weekend."

"How much longer, Law?"

"I can't predict the future, Derringer."

His question keeps bugging me on my drive home. I'm not convinced what I'm seeing from him lately is real. Was he asking how much longer until he gets a shot because he's ready or how much longer he has to keep up an act because it's getting harder for him to behave? It's only been a few weeks.

I want to give him the benefit of the doubt, but my gut says to trust my instincts. And my memories.

Greta's bedroom light glows behind her blinds. She's still up. I sit in my truck for a few minutes, debating whether I should text her or leave her alone tonight. We've spent a lot of time together since the night she lost the bet. I love every minute of it, but she came here for space, and I don't want to smother her.

I kill the engine and walk to my own front door.

When I step out of the shower, my phone lights up at the edge of the sink. I towel off enough to check the notification. It's Greta.

> How'd he do tonight?

>> Surprisingly good. How are you doing tonight?

> It's been productive. But I've run out of things to do . . .

>> If you're trying to hurt my feelings, you should know I'm not too proud to be your last resort.

> Get dressed and come over.

>> Why would I bother getting dressed?

> So you don't have to go back home wearing nothing but a towel in the morning?

>> Again, you've overestimated the depths of my pride.

She doesn't text back, but I hear her laughing on the other side of the wall. I love the way she laughs out loud even when she's alone.

The moment she opens the door, I say, "You look tired."

My regret is consuming, but thankfully, she laughs.

"See, this is why I invited you over. I was feeling pretty good about myself, and I thought, hmm, what would remedy this? And for the record, I am tired."

"What I meant to say was you look beautiful when you're tired."

"Nice towel. You look tired, too, by the way."

"I am. Can I come in?"

She opens the door wider, and I step into her place. It smells like her laundry detergent, fresh and clean. When I hug her, I smell her shampoo, too. She's all soothing scents and body heat.

"You been working tonight?" I ask, still holding her in my arms.

"Yeah, but I'm done. My eyes burn, and I'm pretty sure I don't have any words left in me."

"If I guess what you're working on, will you tell me?"

"Three guesses."

"A novel about a school teacher?"

"No."

"A novel about a woman who seeks revenge on her cheating ex?"

"No."

"Your biography?"

"That would be an autobiography, but also, no. You're all out of guesses."

"Well, damn. What are we going to do now?"

She tiptoes to kiss me, making it much easier to squeeze her ass.

"Have I ever told you what a great ass you have?"

"Every time you have a handful of it."

"Which is not nearly often enough."

"Listen, me and my great ass have shit to do sometimes. We can't just wait around for your squeezes and compliments."

I can't remember the last time a woman made me laugh the way she does. Her ex is an idiot, but I'm glad he cheated. I'm sorry for the pain it caused her, but it's what brought her to me, so I'll always be secretly grateful. Words I'll never let slip from my mouth, no matter how tired I am.

It's hard to believe she's the same woman who flipped me off through her car window. But I'll never forget the fire in her eyes when she did that. I genuinely had no idea what I'd done to piss her off, but when I caught up to her again, a part of me hoped we'd be taking the same exit. When she passed it, I figured I'd never see her again, thought she was probably bound for someplace more exciting.

For once in my life, I actually got lucky.

I scoop her up in my arms and carry her to the bedroom. She looks into my eyes, and I can see the exhaustion in hers, but I see something more there, too. Maybe it's all in my head, but I can't question it because I want too badly to believe this is real. To believe she feels exactly what I'm feeling.

We'll talk about it when she's ready. For now, I'm just going to keep on believing it.

Setting her feet on the floor next to her bed, my eyes linger on her nipples, straining against the soft cotton of her thin tank top.

"You should strip for me sometime."

"How many twenties you got in your wallet right now?"

"Maybe three?"

"Looks like tonight's not sometime." She whips her tank top over her head in one quick maneuver, no teasing gyrations, no build up at all. I drop my towel, and she drops to her knees.

Fuck, the way this woman owns me.

The tip of her hot wet tongue touches the base of my cock, and my balls and my spine tighten in tandem. I look down to watch as she attempts to throat me. Her gag reflex stops her short of the goal, but having her try feels better than the few women in my past who could. She's good. She's so good.

I pull her up before she makes me come. It's late, and we're both too tired to go multiple rounds, and if I'm only going to come once, it's not going to be in her mouth. Or before she comes on mine.

Her hair fans out over her pillow, and her watery eyes and soft smile make me afraid to blink, afraid the tenuous thread that's binding us might break. I know from experience this could all come unraveled in the blink of an eye.

We haven't known each other long enough for these feelings to make sense, but it's already stronger than what I lost before. We'll make sense of it as we go along. I tell myself if it's meant to work, it'll work.

As I kiss my way down her body, all her swells and dips, the tiny scar between her ribs, and every sporadic freckle is familiar. I know every inch of her.

But I barely get a taste before she tugs at my hair. "No. I want to know how it feels to come with you inside me."

"I thought you said it couldn't happen like that for you."

"If I make it happen, it can."

"So, I get a show after all."

"I mean, you can watch, but I'm not doing it for you," she teases.

"Oh, I'm pretty sure watching is going to do it for me."

Her soft whimper when I push inside her sweet pussy is my favorite sound. Her knuckles graze my skin as she moves her hand into position to rub her clit.

I lengthen my strokes to give her more room. "Is this okay?"

"Don't worry about me. Focus on you. Just fuck me the way you would if I'd already come. I'll worry about me."

There's no way I'm not going to worry about her pleasure, and my eyes can't help but be laser-focused on her. The sight of her thin fingers working her clit is so fucking hot. I want to maintain long, slow strokes, but when her fingers circle faster, my pace increases as well.

She rubs frantically as I fuck her harder. Her hips buck, and her back arches beneath me. I could blow right fucking now, but I need her to finish first. She's so close.

I don't want to change anything that might ruin this for her, but goddamn, her pussy keeps getting wetter and hotter and tighter. Looking away helps, but her walls are already squeezing me. I'm not going to be able to hold out for much longer.

I want to talk her through it, but I also don't want to interrupt whatever's going on in her beautiful head right now. Her other hand glides over her chest. When her fingers pause to pinch her nipple, I have to close my eyes.

Not that it helps, because I can still see her swollen pink nipple being squeezed and her glistening clit swelling under her touch . . .

She sucks in a quick breath with a shriek, and I force my eyes back open. I need the image of her coming on my dick for the first time seared into my memory forever.

My restraint shatters while she's still shuddering through the last phase of her orgasm. The spasms of her pussy milking my cock trigger primal instincts. I'm absolutely feral as I fuck my way over the line.

I hope chasing mine didn't cut her release short. I'd hate to think I just experienced something that euphoric while cheating her out of any part of hers. I've never had a bad orgasm, but that was fucking rapturous.

"Sorry if I came too soon."

"Did you come?" she says through ragged breaths. "I didn't notice."

"You finished, right?" I tease back.

She shrugs. "I think I got close."

"If you'd gotten any closer, I'd be trying to revive you right now."

"Did you just admit that you'd have nutted first, and then tried to revive me?"

"I want to say that's not true, but . . ."

I'm lucky she shares my twisted sense of humor. That comment might've been too much for another woman. Not Greta. She laughs along with me, but she pinches my side. I grab her wrist and pull it to my mouth, where I pretend to bite it before I kiss her smooth skin.

I bring her a towel, and then I crawl back into her bed. When she disappears into the bathroom, I know I'm probably going to be asleep by the time she gets back from brushing her teeth. I rearrange her pillows and roll to my side, smiling when I notice the glittery purple pen on her nightstand.

She wanted me to believe she was so hard and no-nonsense when we met, but despite all her heartbreak, she's still drawn to sparkle and shine.

The pen rests on top of a blue notebook, and I know that whatever she's working on is in those pages.

She turns on the shower. She's going to be in there longer than I thought.

I shouldn't look inside. She'll tell me what she's working on when she's ready. It's none of my business.

The notebook is in my hand before I can talk myself out of reaching for it. Propped up on my elbow, I open the cover and flip a few pages. That's all I intend to do, just thumb through, scan a few lines here and there for a quick glimpse into this part of her life.

But some of the pages only have a few lines, some a single paragraph . . . a stanza? Are they poems? She's a poet?

Why wouldn't she tell me that? Did she think I'd make fun of it? Is she ashamed for some reason?

This page is full. Several paragraphs.

And a refrain?

The light from the bathroom spills onto the bed, and my fingers fly off her notebook as if it's burst into flames.

"What are you doing?"

"Are these . . . are you writing songs?"

"Why would you open that?"

"Why wouldn't you tell me? Can I keep reading?"

"No, you can't! You need to leave."

"Greta, come on—"

"Get out, Law."

Fuuuuuuuck!

18

Greta

But Why?

I thought I was done crying myself to sleep, swallowing sobs so Law wouldn't hear me through the wall, but I did it again after he left my bed last night. I hate that I did it at all, but it's so much worse knowing he was the cause of my tears. I should still be cursing his name, so full of anger I can't see straight, but the anger didn't last long at all.

The feeling that remains isn't great, though.

Daylight's blasting in through my blinds, and I know it's not early, but I don't want to look at the time or check my messages or even be awake, for that matter.

I want to go back to sleep and pretend last night ended some other way. Or to just be able to magically let it go so we can get back to what I think we were becoming. I don't really want to let it go, but it would be easier than what I'm feeling right now.

He shouldn't have read my notebook without asking, but it's not like it was a journal filled with all my personal thoughts and feelings. It still feels like such a betrayal, like he did something so much worse than just reading some half-assed lyrics.

Am I rationalizing or being logical? I don't even know.

But I'm not backsliding into days like this, lying in bed, feeling stupid. I didn't come here looking for a relationship. If there was something building between us and it imploded this early, then it wouldn't have lasted, anyway. It's too soon for me to jump into something new to begin with.

I came here to find my strength, to recover my independence.

I'd start with feeding myself if I thought I could eat. My car needs an oil change. Law told me not to pay anyone to do it, said he'd do it this weekend.

This weekend clearly went off-script, so I either need to take my car somewhere and pay someone to change the oil or learn how to do it myself. How hard could it be?

The internet comes in clutch with dozens of videos on how to change the oil in a car. But it turns out, it's not the same for every car, and I just wasted an hour rewatching the same video three times before I realized this.

Why can't I be one of those people who watches a video one time and gets it? My head hurts, and I'm not in the mood to watch another damn video over and over again. I think I've got the gist of it. I'll figure it out.

I'm staring under the hood of my car when Law's voice registers in my ear. What did he say? Reluctantly, I look in his direction.

He's standing in his yard, staring at me.

"What are you doing?"

"An oil change."

"Telepathically?"

I glare in his general direction. "You're not always as funny as you think you are."

He walks toward me, and I wish that didn't make me want to run inside and hide from him. I stand my ground.

"I told you I'd change your oil, Greta."

"Yeah, well, you said a lot of things."

"None of them lies. I know you're mad at me, and you have every right to be, but let me at least make good on my promise to change your oil, okay?"

"It wasn't exactly a promise."

"I considered it one. I'm changing your oil."

"Fine! Knock yourself out. Change the damn oil." I throw my arms up, storm inside and slam the door. Not my finest moment, but then again, opening that notebook damn sure wasn't his either.

I can hear him out there clanging tools around. It sounds excessive for an oil change, if you ask me. And what am I supposed to do now? I'm trapped.

Is he talking to himself out there?

A quick peek through my blinds reveals there is actually someone else on our shared driveway. And now, Law's yelling at him. He's probably taking all his frustration with me out on that poor kid.

I march back outside. "Whoa. Whoa. Whoa. Take it down a notch!"

The young man looks shocked to see me. He's probably so embarrassed.

"Hi," I say, extending my hand. "I'm Greta."

"It's nice to meet you." He timidly shakes my hand. "I'm Derringer."

This is the infamous Derringer Wells? He looks like a complete sweetheart with his sandy blonde, shaggy hair and his big, green eyes –a little bit like a much younger and taller Keith Urban. I can see the heartthrob aspect, but not the reckless bad boy that Law's made him out to be.

"Law's told me so much about you."

He drops his head, and I see bruises and scrapes on his cheek and his jaw. I just want to hug him. It's obvious he knows Law hasn't said great things about him, and clearly, something bad has happened to him.

"I'll let you get back to your car repairs," he says quietly to Law. "I guess call me later. If you want. I can tell you the rest."

"I'm pretty sure I've heard enough."

Derringer nods, and then he walks off to a waiting car. The young woman behind the wheel looks worried.

After they drive away, I turn to Law. "What's going on with him?"

"Well, he no longer has a truck, and he's probably lucky to be alive."

"He wrecked it?"

"Says he's sure it's totaled." He aggressively screws the lid back on an empty plastic oil bottle before he throws it at the ground. It bounces up at an angle, and then ricochets off the garage door.

"Did you make sure he's physically okay? His face is cut up and bruised. He probably has other injuries."

"I'm not a doctor."

"Has he seen one?"

"I don't know. And I don't fucking care. He wants to piss away his future, there's nothing I can do about that."

"He's just a kid, Law."

"He's twenty-one-years-old."

"And you and I both know that's only an adult on paper. He's a kid. Didn't you make mistakes at that age?"

"We've had this conversation."

"No, I don't think we have. You side-stepped it when I brought it up before."

"I had extenuating circumstances for my mistakes."

"Maybe he does, too. You said you don't think he's close to his family. What's the story there?"

"I don't know."

"What do you mean you don't know?"

"I'm not his guardian. I've done all I can do for him."

"Well, I haven't. He looks like he could use a home-cooked meal with friends. Invite him over tonight. I'll have dinner ready at six."

"Am I also supposed to come to this dinner?"

"I'd imagine it would be pretty damn uncomfortable for him to have dinner at my place without you, don't you think?"

"You have a good heart, Greta, but what he needs right now is some tough love."

"You've already tried that. And from what I can tell, it doesn't seem to be working."

"Greta—"

"I shouldn't even be speaking to you right now, let alone inviting you to dinner! And you're trying to get out of it?"

"No, ma'am. See you at six."

"Bring wine, not beer."

"Alcohol might be the last thing he needs."

"Never said I planned on sharing."

I repeat my earlier performance of storming inside and slamming the door. Shit. If I'm cooking dinner for three tonight, I need to go to the grocery store.

With the door open just enough to peek my head out, I yell, "Let me know when my car is drivable again! I've got errands to run!"

He salutes me like a soldier.

I should go back out there and . . .

Grrrrrr! He can be such an insufferable ass, I swear!

At this rate, my door is going to need new hinges before I get dinner on the table.

19

Law

Dinner Talk

She's pushing my buttons with this whole family dinner thing. I bought the wine, but this is a bad idea. I'm only going through with it because I want her to see that I'm not actually a bad person. I just apparently still make mistakes at thirty-two. She won't let me explain, but if I can show her that I'm better than that . . .

But she needs a bigger reality check where Derringer is concerned. When it comes to him, she's the one who's making a mistake.

Opening that notebook was an invasion of her privacy, but she's invading my professional life here. If she and I were in a different place, I'd tell her how inappropriate this is, but right now, she has fresh ammunition to fire back about my inappropriate behavior.

We'd just end up in a fight, and a fight is exactly what I'm trying to avoid. She wouldn't believe me about him, anyway. She needs to see for herself.

If sitting down to dinner with Derringer is what it takes to make her happy, I'll bring the wine and check my professional opinion at the door.

This isn't a business dinner where I'm trying to get to know a musician better. I know all I need to know about this kid. Greta will know soon enough, but I won't say I told you so.

I'll think it, but I won't say it.

Here goes nothing.

"You're early," she says, looking me up and down like she's weighing whether or not to let me in.

"You said six. It's five-forty-five. Fifteen minutes early is on time."

"Oh yeah, I forgot you're one of those people."

Let it go, Law. Let it go.

"I brought wine."

She takes the bottle and walks back toward her kitchen. I step inside, but instead of her laundry detergent or her shampoo or perfume, I smell my mom's pot roast.

Or Greta's, apparently.

When she cooked for me, I got grocery store pizza. For Derringer, she makes this?

I'm not complaining about that pizza. The night we ate that pizza is my favorite memory. Everything that came before and after that pizza, I would very much like to experience again. But if I have a shot in hell at maintaining any of that in my life, I've got to repair the damage I've done.

And her other damaged dinner guest just knocked on the door.

"Can you let him in, please?"

"Sure."

My pleasure. Can't think of anything I'd rather do right now.

He stands on her doorstep, holding two bottles of wine, one white and one red.

"Hey," he says. "I wasn't sure if your girlfriend liked red or white, so I brought both. Is that okay? She doesn't hate wine or anything, does she?"

He's genuinely nervous. Huh, I didn't know the cocky little shit had it in him. I don't correct him on the girlfriend assumption.

"She usually drinks red, but if she doesn't want the white, maybe you can take it back home to your driver." I step aside to let him in as the car that dropped him off pulls away. "Is she not joining us?"

"Oh, I didn't know if I should bring anyone. You didn't say, and I didn't want to assume anything." He shrugs. "She's going to pick me up in a few hours, unless I need to text her sooner."

"Is that the same girl who was hanging on your arm when I left you at the bar?"

"Yeah. Whitley. She's great."

"Party girls always are. In the beginning."

"She's not, though. We only had one drink before we left the bar. That's not her deal."

"Roads were dry. Summer, so you can't blame ice on the road. You expect me to believe you blacked out while sober?"

"No. I was fully awake, just being stupid. Going too fast and not paying attention. My right front tire went off the road. No shoulder and more of a drop-off than I realized. I lost control while I was trying to get back up on the pavement. Rolled it. Twice."

"Was Whitley in the truck with you?"

He stares at his boots. "Yeah." Before he looks back up to meet my eyes, he shakes his head hard. "I know we got lucky."

"That only happens so many times in one life."

"I know. And I know you probably don't believe me, but—"

Greta comes bounding over like she's just realized he was here.

"Derringer, hi. I'm so glad you could come."

"Thanks for having me." He holds out the bottles he's brought. "I-I didn't know if you preferred red or white."

"Aw, I was just saying I should've thought to get wine. And here you are, being the perfect guest. That's so sweet. Thank you. Come to the table. Dinner's ready."

Excuse me? I brought wine first! And I bet it's a nicer bottle than either of the ones he just handed you.

Let it go, Law. Let it go.

Her pot roast is fucking amazing. And so are her small talk skills. You'd think I'd be better at that, given my line of work. But I've never been much for mindless chit-chat. I've been told I can come off abrasive. It's never my intention.

If the situation is business, I like to get to the point. If it's personal, I'd rather have a real conversation about something that matters.

She's got Derringer going on and on about how he got into music. He's spooling out all his childhood memories for her. Started piano lessons when he was four. Got his first guitar when he was seven. His dad would let him busk downtown in front of the Pecan Tree Café, while he was inside signing real estate contracts and mineral leases.

"He liked to do business in public back then," Derringer clarifies. "Always liked feeling important. These days, he spends more time on his plane, flying to Fort Worth or Houston nearly every week."

A kid from the wealthiest family in the area, playing for change on the sidewalk while his dad was in a corner booth, being important. I bet people wagged their tongues plenty about that. The Wells family is still a favorite subject of gossip in this town.

And I can feel for Derringer having to grow up in that spotlight, but he's grown now, and he contributes his own material.

"Yeah, I heard your family was in the oil business," Greta says.

"They make sure everyone hears that."

"You're not interested in following in their footsteps, I take it."

"No, ma'am. Not in the least. I know I had a lot of advantages growing up because of oil money, but I know enough about that business to know it's not for me."

"Your dad has his own plane? If he flies that often, it seems like it would be easier to move closer to the big cities."

"The land we live on has been in the Wells family for generations. Plus, if he moved to a bigger city, he might not be so important."

"Ah, big fish, little pond."

"Yes, ma'am. This roast is really good."

"I'm glad you're enjoying it."

I've been watching them talk without contributing at all. I'm sure Greta's making note of that. I better chime in.

"I bet your parents would prefer you to stay out of dancehalls and get back into classrooms."

He shrugs. "College wasn't for me. They didn't want me to go because it would teach me about the family business, anyway. Trust me, they planned on handling that education behind closed doors. The only reason they wanted me to go to college was for appearances. I was supposed to get the degree to hang on the wall, and make all the right connections."

"You might need connections in the music industry, too."

"I might like those people a whole lot better."

Damn. For the first time ever, I hear real conviction in his voice. He knows what he doesn't want. If he held that much conviction about what he does want, his chances would be a whole lot better.

"I think there might be more similarities in the two businesses than you realize," I say. "There's competition. Both can probably feel a little cut-throat at times. Chance plays a bigger role than people like to admit. You can be a big deal one day, and forgotten the next."

"Yeah, and any industry can have its share of dirty deals being made, too. But until all the deals are dirty in the music business, the similarities are more limited than you know."

"I'm sure there are good people working in the oil industry."

"Of course there are. But they might be working for someone less good, whether they know it or not."

Greta's looking at me with so much *I told you so* in her eyes right now, but I don't know what any of this has to do with Derringer's lack of commitment. In fact, if he's that opposed to the family business, you'd think he'd be ten times more serious about developing all that talent he's wasting. I actually can't think of anything more motivating than a predetermined life you don't want. Hell, he should be so desperate to prove his way off that path I'd have to remind him to get out and enjoy his youth before it's too late.

Nobody has to remind this kid to enjoy a damn thing.

He's enjoying the hell out of this meal.

And Greta is enjoying the speech she's writing in her head—the one she's going to unleash on me as soon as he's gone. I can see the purple glittery pen in her head flying across a page I won't have to sneak to read. She's going to be all too eager to share every word of it with me.

I sense a lot of verbal punctuation coming on. And the way she makes her eyes so big when she's fired up. Hand gestures. She's never going to leave those out.

20

Greta

Ready or Not

The front door is barely closed behind Derringer before I have to let it out. "Still think you're so right about him?"

Law takes a deep breath. "I know what you want me to say here, but I also know you value honesty. So, yeah. I still think he's not ready, and I still doubt his big break is ever going to come because I'm not convinced that he'll ever be ready."

"He might not need you. You've thought of that, right?"

"I have. And if someone else can save him from himself, then they deserve to sign him. They can claim to have discovered him, and he can write me out of his story completely. Honestly, nothing would make me happier than to be wrong about him, but I can't keep pouring so much energy into someone who doesn't know what to do with it and won't listen when I try to tell him."

"Maybe if you tried in a softer voice, Law."

"A softer fucking voice? What do you want me to do, whisper sweet nothings in his ear?"

I glare, and I hope he knows he's on thin ice here.

"The last thing I want to do is let you down again," he says. "But I don't see a softer voice reaching him."

"We're not talking about me and you."

"I want to. Can we?"

"I don't know, Law. Are you ready?"

"Yeah, why wouldn't I be ready?"

"Because I have questions. And I'm not sure you're willing to answer them, but if you want to talk about the possibility of there being an us, then I need you to be ready to do that."

"Ask me whatever you want to know."

"Why do you always say you know so much about Derringer when you don't seem to know anything about him at all?"

He sits on my couch with his elbows on his knees and his head in his hands. Finally, he looks up and spits it out. "I got signed at his age."

"Signed to do what? Baseball?"

"No, Greta. I didn't play baseball. I played guitar and sang. Just like Derringer. Well, not just like him because there are few people who have ever picked up a guitar and stepped up to a mic who are as good as he is. He's got a voice that stands out from a sea of talented voices. They're all similar. He's unique. But those similar voices that aren't nearly as good? They've got a far better shot because they've got more than just the voice. The voice alone isn't enough. Not even a voice like his. The reality is that people far less talented than him are going to accomplish a hell of a lot more."

"You're a singer?"

"I was."

"What happened?"

"I was madly in love by the time I got the deal. On top of the world after. We moved to Nashville and found a one-bedroom apartment that felt like a pitstop on our way to a mansion. But it didn't happen as fast for me as we thought it would. And I was to blame for most of the delays. I bought into my own hype, and thought I knew more than I did. Thought I knew more than everybody did."

"And?"

"And she got tired of waiting. She met someone who understood things I didn't, someone who knew how to actually take control of a career while mine was spinning out of control. She got her mansion."

"And then what?"

"I quit. Gave up."

"Please tell me you are fucking joking! Some gold digger walked out on you, and you just gave up on life?"

"She had aspirations that included wealth, yes, but blaming her for my choices isn't fair. I know now that she and I never would've lasted, but I was young and in love. It was the realest thing I'd ever known. When I lost her, I thought I was losing everything that mattered. The truth is I knew I'd already fucked up so much more. I was scared and confused and heartbroken. I wasn't ready, Greta. Not for any of it."

"You never wanted to try again?"

"Some chances only come along once in a lifetime."

"That sounds like some cop-out bullshit to me."

"What happened to kindness and understanding? Softer voices?"

"I think you need tough love more than you need any of that."

"Is that right?"

"Yeah. I am right. Derringer has made mistakes, but you're projecting yours onto him, and that's not fair."

"There's more to it than that. I know what it takes to make it, and it's hard at any age. But he needs a few more years of the real world before he takes that leap. He's not ready. If he gets his shot now, he'll fuck it up."

"Maybe he wouldn't if someone believed in him enough. Even if he did fail on the first try, he might have the guts to try again. And he might not fail the second time out. Not everybody lassoes the stars on their first attempt, Law."

"You about done?"

"Are you?"

"What are you asking me, if I'm done listening to you call me gutless or done babysitting Derringer?"

"It doesn't even occur to you that the question might've been about you? Just you? Not you in relation to me or you in relation to Derringer?"

"All I know is I don't want to be done with you. I don't know why you would be willing to give anyone a second chance after what you've been through, but I want one. So, this is me asking, can I try again with you? Will you try again with me?"

"We still have a lot to learn about each other."

"We do, but we've learned a lot in the past twenty-four hours. We both had a secret. I used to be a singer, and you write songs."

"I bet you could be a singer again, if you wanted to. And I'm not a real songwriter. I'm actually the last person in the world who should be writing songs. I know nothing about music. I can't read it. I can't write it. The best I could do is hum to give someone an idea of what I have in mind, and even that would be terrible, because did I mention I also can't sing? I can't carry a tune. Can't recognize a chord or name it . . .

"But I understand people and emotions, and I just have this strong pull to write about that. And I don't know why I need my words to be lyrics instead of short stories or novels or poems for the sake of poetry, but that's all I can see them as. Lyrics. With no music."

"Huh. If only you knew a guy who knew something about music."

"Are you saying you want us to write songs together?"

"I'm saying I'm willing to give it a try if you are. But you'd have to actually show me the lyrics."

The way this possibility makes me feel is not like me at all. As if a switch just flipped inside me, I say, "Okay. Yeah. Let's take a chance on each other."

He pulls me onto his lap and kisses me. His hands are in my hair, and there's such a natural rhythm to our kiss that I'm sure every kiss before I met him had to have been bad, even the ones that seemed great at the time.

I don't want to let my guard down too much yet, but I melt into his kiss. This is the kiss that made me believe in second chances. How does something so fundamental change so fast and so entirely?

His sudden stark honesty stripped away layers—of what I don't know, but it's all gone.

When the kiss breaks and I look into his eyes, I know he's not gutless. It took courage to admit how he feels and ask me to try again. I want to write songs with him, but I want to hear him sing, too.

"I promise I'm not putting any conditions on us when I ask you this, but will you get on stage again? Even just one night somewhere local, so I can hear you sing?"

"Yeah, I'll sing for you."

"And will you please hang in there with Derringer for a little while longer?"

I know that look. That look tells me I'm pushing my luck, but I had to ask.

"I still think I'm right about him, Greta. But I can't fucking say no to you."

Lying awake later that night in my bed alone, I hear a guitar being randomly strummed. I'm no musician, but I know he's tuning a guitar on his side of the wall. I've never heard him playing a guitar over there. But he's playing now, so I close my eyes and listen. I don't recognize the song, but I like it. It's soothing. Things are changing on both sides of our shared wall.

21

Lav

Gotta Get It Right

I've been working on it for a few weeks, but I'm still trying to nail the composition for "The Way I Love the Dark." In my defense, it's still baseball season.

And I keep staring at games that I have zero interest in because I need to get this perfect. I keep getting close, but it's not there yet. Reading these lyrics without her permission is the reason I nearly lost her. Now, she's listening to my input, letting me tweak words. Every time I read through them again, I like them even more.

And I'm more grateful every time that something good came out of my mistake.

She's a lyricist, and I'm a musician, and together, I know we could create great songs. But I didn't realize how much pressure I'd feel trying to put music to lyrics she wrote on her own.

I keep telling myself the breakthrough I need is coming.

Greta knocks, and I yell, "It's open." I've told her over and over again she doesn't have to knock.

Her hair is up in a clip to keep it off her neck in this heat, but there are a few stray pieces stuck to her forehead. She left to go run errands while I was mowing the grass this morning. She's probably hoping I have something new to play for her.

"I haven't made much headway."

"Does working with your hands ever help unlock your musical genius?"

"What did you break?"

"I started doing laundry before I left this morning, but the warning light on my dryer came on. It says *check vent*. I always clean the lint screen, and the dryer hasn't been moved, so I don't know why there would suddenly be a problem with the vent, but I stopped using it, just in case. I'd call the landlord, but we both know—"

"He'll take days to get back to you. The hose is probably loose. I'll come look at it."

She stares at the open composition book on my coffee table and bites her bottom lip. "I should probably tell you something."

"Do I need to sit back down for this?"

"No. I don't think so. But I've written some new lyrics."

"That's great. When I said I wanted us to collaborate more, I didn't mean you shouldn't write on your own at all anymore. I'll take a look at the dryer, and then you can show me your new verses. I just made some tea. You want a glass?"

"No. I've had too much caffeine today already."

"Well, if I'd known you were at the coffee shop, I would've known to expect new lyrics."

"I can't help it. That place is like magic."

"You're the magic, Greta. That place just has cake."

"Magic cake."

Her dryer hose has not only come loose, it's crimped and split. This thing is probably older than her car. Cheap part, easy fix. No need to go through our unreliable landlord for this.

"I'm going to get you a new dryer hose. Do you want to go to dinner when I'm done installing it?"

"Or we could order pizza and eat here while I share the new song with you."

"It's a whole song?"

"Maybe."

"I'll take that as a yes, so yes to pizza." Looking at fresh lyrics might loosen me up.

The hardest part of replacing the hose is moving the dryer away from the wall and squeezing into the tight space to work. Her warning light's back off, and her clothes are tumbling again. Time to grab a shower and clear my head for her new song.

"So, what's this new song about?" I ask as we pull our first slices from the box.

"Well, you know how Derringer opened up about his family over dinner? About how he feels about the way they do business?"

"He alluded to some things, yeah."

"Right. And those things kept coming back to me."

"You wrote this song with him in mind?"

"Yeah, but I'd never want him to feel like I'm trying to put words in his mouth, you know? He inspired it, but I'm not trying to tell his story. And I know I could've gotten it totally wrong and he may hate it, but—"

"Let me see it."

"I wasn't trying to presume to know things I don't. But the chorus sort of wrote itself, and it wouldn't leave me alone."

"Greta, I can't participate in this conversation if I don't know what we're talking about."

She takes a deep breath. "I know. Maybe we should finish eating first."

"I can multitask. Hand me the notebook."

"If it sucks, just say that, okay? I can take it."

I chew without talking, let her keep rambling until her nervous energy winds down enough for me to get another word in edgewise. Wiping my hands on a paper towel, I try again, "Are you ready to let me see it now?"

"No, but I'll never be ready. So, here." She passes the notebook over the pizza.

My eyes scan the page, skimming to find the chorus she said grabbed hold and wouldn't let her go. Seems like I should start with that and work my way back over the whole piece.

They never got their hands dirty, but shook dirty hands...

I read the chorus several times before I work through it from the top. She said the chorus wrote itself. The composition is already starting to flow that way, too, but this song . . . it doesn't feel presumptuous. It feels momentous.

And like it could prove disastrous for an artist from old oil money. These are words that could sever bonds.

"Damn, Greta. I wasn't expecting this. Your other two songs are heavy with emotion, but not in this way. Even if it's not exactly his story . . . him singing this? I don't know."

"Is it all wrong for his voice?"

"Shit. That's right. You've never heard him sing. He's playing tonight. You should hear him. He goes on at ten."

"Yikes. I forgot people go out that late."

"If I can do it at thirty-two, you can do it at twenty-eight."

"Maybe this is a good night for me to hear you both sing. I bet he wouldn't mind sharing the stage with you for a little while."

"Oh, you're just full of good ideas, aren't you?"

"This started as your idea, remember?"

"No. It was your ideas that started it."

I read over the lyrics several more times while she gets ready. And they're more unsettling with each read-through. Words that can shake people up are the ones that'll stick, for better or for worse. I tell myself it's just a song, and the choice would ultimately be his.

So help me, I thought I was done with Derringer Wells. But she just had to go and ask me to stick with him, and then she put this song in my hands.

She's never even heard his voice. She has no idea, yet somehow, she knew.

There's wisdom in these lyrics, but near accusations, too. Some not-so-subtle insinuations.

I used to trust my gut without question when it came to singers and songs, but this makes me think maybe I've aged out of the game. There was a time when I wouldn't have worried about repercussions.

If people want you to write good things about them, they should be good people, right? Otherwise, they get what they get.

But what does it get the one who crosses the line and sings the song? Ultimately, in the end, what does he get if he sings this?

There is no doubt in my mind what he'll say when he sees these lyrics.

We don't have to go there tonight, though. Tonight, she'll hear him sing someone else's songs. And then we'll work on hers together until we get it just right.

Whether it's right for him or not is a question that can wait. I start over at the top and read it one more time.

The Song That Changed Everything

BETWEEN THE CRUDE AND THE NEON

I'm from a long line of tall men with loud mouths
They say loyalty matters and blood is the glue
But all that's left in their veins is that west Texas crude

It built all their walls, defined them and refined them
And oiled the narrow path they put me on
But it was clear from the jump, I . . .
Well, I was more drawn to the neon

They never got their hands dirty, but shook dirty hands
No busted knuckles, but there's blood on their land
I was born with their name, but not meant for that life
Night after night, I'm out here chasing a new one
Stuck somewhere between the crude and the neon

Busted some knuckles and done some things wrong
Fighting somewhere between the crude and the neon

They gilded the way, said the road never ends
But I'm the detour where it all goes wrong
Their lost black sheep confessing in songs

I've made some mistakes and got some regrets
But I know their legacy ain't as good as it gets
So I'll refuse all their offers and keep singing my song
Running from the crude while chasing the neon

They say in the end, it's family that counts
Well, I'd rather count on this family I've found
One sells by the barrel and one buys a round
And I'm a whole lot prouder of this family I've found

They never got their hands dirty, but shook dirty hands
No busted knuckles, but there's blood on their land
I was born with their name, but not meant for that life
Night after night, I'm out here chasing a new one
Stuck somewhere between the crude and the neon

My dreams haven't hit but I'm hangin' on
Out here somewhere between the crude and the neon

22

Greta

REASON TO CELEBRATE

I insist on opening the champagne myself, and yes, I know how to open it so the cork doesn't pop off and create a geyser. But I let this one fly. It's a moment deserving of dramatic recognition.

Law has finally conceded that he's finished with the composition for "Between the Crude and the Neon."

This bottle has been chilling in my fridge for days, waiting for him to accept that he's done. That it's not just good enough, it's good.

He hasn't tweaked anything in over a week. I knew the exact moment he nailed it, but he's played it on his guitar a thousand more times and sung it until I'm almost sick of hearing it. It sounds too good in his voice for me to ever really get sick of it.

Ever since I heard him sing for the first time, I've known that he should've never given up. If Derringer doesn't want to sing this song, Law definitely could.

It wouldn't matter that it's not about his lived experience. People sing the hell out of lyrics that have nothing to do with their actual lives all the time. I'm the one who wrote the lyrics, and they couldn't be any more removed from my real life.

Before we show the song to Derringer or consider what comes next if he loves it or he doesn't, we have to celebrate this moment because Law and I did this. We're still fiddling with the lyrics and the music for "The Way I Love the Dark" and my other song that doesn't even have a name, but this one is done. This is our first.

He watches the flow of champagne spewing over my hands and shakes his head.

"I told you to let me do it."

"No way. You would've made it all anti-climactic."

"As opposed to the mess you've made."

"Oh, this won't be the last mess I make for you."

His eyebrows shoot up, and the words replay in my head. I hear it now, but all I meant was that I'm going to keep being me, which is probably going to keep driving him crazy because there are always going to be things we don't agree on, but my messes will be worth it, and his obsessive need for perfection might make me crazy, too, but—

This kiss will always be the reminder. We work. We're good together. Whether it's too soon by traditional standards or not, and no matter how different our ways, the things I feel when he kisses me like this are the realest, brightest feelings, and they make anything I thought I knew in the past irrelevant.

I know things now that I never knew before, like the truth that how long you've known someone isn't the validation people make it out to be. It's timing that makes the difference, not length of time.

This kiss seals the deal. Every time.

And this song is a wrap. Sealed with a kiss. Done.

"We need glasses," I murmur against his mouth. "We have to toast."

"Why not just chug it straight from the bottle at this point?"

When will he learn? I turn up the bottle and drink, filling my mouth too quickly with champagne. The bubbles become foam, shock becomes laughter, and my mouth becomes a fountain just like the bottle when I opened it.

He laughs with me this time. "Are you sure you're ready for this?"

"I honestly have no idea. But if I sit around worrying about whether or not I'm ready instead of going for it, I'll never know, will I? You never really know if you're ready for anything until you try."

"You're not nervous at all?" he asks.

"Of course, I'm nervous. But before I shared this with you, I was scared shitless. You took one look and said, 'this could work,' and I believed you. Do you still believe that?"

"I do still believe that. I also believe you are covered in champagne. And someone should clean you up."

"It's all over you, too."

"Then I guess we'll have to clean each other."

"I think I'm probably the messiest so—"

"You know I plan on taking care of you first."

"Lead the way."

"Bring the bottle."

His hot tongue licks drying champagne from my chest, clearing a path through the stickiness on my skin as his mouth moves closer to my nipple.

My fingers trail through his hair. "I'm not sure this is how all songwriting duos celebrate, but it could definitely be the reward that motivates me to keep writing."

"Better than chocolate?"

"Chocolate, champagne, and you. I'll take that trifecta all day every day."

"You want it all, huh?"

"Always."

He sinks his thick cock into my drenched pussy, pushing his hips forward until he's fully sheathed while his mouth encases the hardened peak his tongue has been teasing.

Yeah, I want it all. Always.

The bulb in my bedside lamp flickers before it goes out completely right as the washing machine buzzes to let me know my clothes are ready for the dryer, momentarily drowning out the monotonous tune of the ice cream truck filtering in from the street. All around us, it's just another ordinary Saturday afternoon, but here we are, doing unseen extraordinary things in this completely unremarkable place.

I push against his shoulders and shift to my side to let him know I want to change positions. He goes up onto his knees to allow me to flip over, but I shake my head and smile.

"No. It's my turn to be on top."

Sitting tall, I circle my hips until I feel his dick pulse and my walls do the same. I lean forward and grab the champagne bottle from the nightstand, bringing it to my lips when I resume my position.

Taking a slow, measured drink, I savor every sensation—the gentle tingling as tiny bubbles fizz on my tongue before I swallow, the firmness of his hips between my thighs as I rock forward and back, fucking him like he belongs to me, even as his gaze elicits goosebumps over my skin because he owns me, too.

We've become intertwined in ways that give over parts of ourselves to each other. My lyrics don't work without his music, but my anger didn't fade until it brushed up against his stubbornness either. And it wouldn't have fallen away to let my secret dream flourish if I hadn't seen the embers of his ambition still smoldering behind all his headstrong avoidance. He's still avoiding it, but I see it.

I take another drink, and tilt my head back to let the bubbles slide down my throat. I feel light and unburdened. Sexy and desired. Capable and trusted.

He's smiling up at me when I glance down to make sure he's still watching. I don't think he's taken his eyes off me since he walked through my door.

Without considering if I should or not, I just say the words.

"I love you."

"I fucking adore you, Greta. I've loved you since before you could tell the difference between a ball and strike."

"We're going to be incredible."

"We already are."

23
Law

THE AGATE RIDGE SESSION

At Greta's insistence, Derringer brings Whitley with him to dinner this time.

She's still anxious about showing him the song, but cooking seems to be her favorite outlet for anxiety. I never would've dreamed the woman who forgot to turn the oven on for a pizza was actually such a damn good cook.

There's a lot I wouldn't have dreamed back then.

He shows up with two bottles of wine again, one red and one white. "I figured why break tradition, right?"

Greta beams as she accepts the bottles. He's got almost as much charm as he does talent. It's probably kept him out of some trouble he deserved, despite all the trouble he found. He hasn't missed a show time in a couple of months now. Insurance paid off his old truck. Access to family money ensured he got all the extras possible on the new one.

That's not likely to happen again if he records the song that we're finally ready to share with him. They really might cut him off completely. Then again, if my instincts still count for anything, he won't need anyone to help him buy him anything else if he can keep his nose clean and keep charming a crowd.

The kid's on his way, whether he's ready or not. If I don't get him signed, someone else will.

Whitley brought a cake for dessert. It's not until she lifts the lid on the box that we see it's a birthday cake. She pulls two candles from her purse and pushes them into the frosting.

Derringer shakes his head like he's embarrassed, but he's not fooling anybody in the room. He loves the attention. "I didn't know you brought candles."

"Twenty-two, huh?" I feel like I should've known it was his birthday. There was a time it wouldn't have occurred to me to feel bad about not knowing something like that. I can definitely chalk that change up to Greta's influence.

"And a whole lot wiser than I was at twenty-one."

"But still plenty dumb," I assure him.

He laughs. "All right. But if I keep getting wiser every year, maybe someday I'll be as smart as you."

"Put a lid on the charming bullshit. It's not going to work on me." I shake his hand and wish him a sincere happy birthday. "Are you opposed to talking business on your birthday?"

His face lights up, and I know what he's expecting. But before we get to that...

"Greta is not only an amazing host, she's a songwriter."

"Oh yeah? Anything I might know?"

She shakes her head. "Not yet. But you were the inspiration for one. I'm not really a songwriter, just the lyrics. Lucky for me, I know a music man, one who saw some promise in my lyrics and put a whole lot of effort into making them more than I could've imagined. He's the reason it's a song."

"And she's downplaying her own talent, but you'll recognize that as soon as you hear it."

"Before you hear it," she says. "I need you to know that I wasn't trying to pretend to know your life, Derringer. Your stories at dinner just set the wheels in motion, and I wrote what I wrote. You inspired it, but I never meant in any way to—"

"We're going to be here all night if you don't tell her to stop talking so you can hear the damn song and decide for yourself how you feel about it."

His smile is sheepish. "With all due respect, Greta, I think I would like to hear this song."

"We should sing Happy Birthday first," she counters.

Now, even Whitley shakes her head. "We can do that later."

I open my notebook to the whole song and hand it to Derringer. And then, with my guitar across my lap, I introduce him to it live.

He looks back and forth between me and the page, wide-eyed and slack-jawed, until the last note is played. And then he looks directly at Greta. "It's like you pulled these words from my soul. Would you let me sing this?"

"That's why we're sharing it with you," I say. "With the hope that you might want to sing it. But I want you to consider the consequences you might face before you commit to anything."

"Definitely," Greta says. "We don't want to encourage anything that would hurt your relationship with your family."

"No, ma'am. If family ties can't withstand a song that tells my truth, well, that's on them. Not you. I'd be honored to sing this song. Hell, I'm dying to sing this song. Honestly, it deserves more exposure than it'll get with me, though."

I set my guitar aside. "If I told you I was ready to bring the necessary people to the table to increase your exposure, would you show up for that meeting?"

"When?"

"Tomorrow at two."

"I'll be there at one-forty-five."

"Right answer."

"Where do we meet?" he asks, unable to keep the trembling excitement out of his voice.

"I was thinking the Pecan Street Café."

"Yeah, that feels right." He smiles like a seven-year-old-kid with a brand-new guitar.

"I guess the only thing left to do tonight is cut the cake and sing Happy Birthday to your lucky ass."

We sing the song and cut the cake. And then Derringer sits on Greta's couch, borrows my guitar, and gives us a private performance that none of us will ever forget.

24

Greta

No More Detours

I do a final sweep through my side of the duplex. It's as empty as the day I moved in. Law honks his horn in the driveway, so I sit right down in the middle of the living room floor and take a few more moments to appreciate all the changes that happened here. Never thought I'd be leaving so soon.

Never expected anything at all about my time here to go the way that it did.

And the changes keep coming.

I climb up into the truck, and his exasperated expression morphs into a smile. "No regrets about selling your car?"

"Oh, yeah. I don't know what I'll do without the constant fear of where I'll be stranded when it breaks down next."

He leans over for a kiss. "We'll get you into a new car as soon as we have an address to put on the paperwork."

"We've got a long list of places to look at."

"I don't doubt that for a minute. You ready to put Agate Ridge, Texas in the rearview mirror?"

"I'm ready."

Our last kiss on the driveway where we officially met lingers. I think we're both feeling a little nostalgic about how this all got started. But it's time.

"I'll navigate," I say, reaching for his phone mount and turning the screen toward me.

"No, thanks. I've seen your navigation skills." He repositions his phone exactly like he had it before I got in. "You'll have us missing all our exits."

"I've only missed one exit in my entire life, and that was your fault."

He puts the truck in reverse and backs away from our first shared address, where I was A and he was B, even though he got here before me. "The fact that you still believe I caused you to miss that exit is further proof you should not be trusted to navigate."

"Hey, remember this?" I flip him off from the passenger seat.

"Aw, there's that sweet girl who stole my heart on the interstate."

"Says the insufferable ass who cut me off."

"One last trip to Coffee and Cake?"

"You distract them while I steal the fake monstera."

"Sorry, we're on a schedule here. I don't have time to bail you out of jail. You're going to have to settle for caffeine and a slice of cake."

"I can't wait until we have our rambling old farmhouse fully restored, and I can fill it with plants."

"You keep ignoring me when I say this, but we are not buying a fixer-upper."

"Listen, I promise not to sleep with any of our contractors while you're on tour."

"Me going on tour at this stage is magical thinking, sweetheart."

"Lucky for you, I'm really good at that."

"You are definitely good." He pulls my hand to his mouth and pretends to bite it before he kisses my fingers "And I know exactly how lucky I am."

"Take me to Nashville, you road raging psychopath."

25

Greta

ONE YEAR LATER...

Law wrestles with the pocket door between our primary bedroom and bathroom again. If he'd open it with patience, it wouldn't get stuck, but I've given up trying to convince him.

"Dammit, Greta. We have got to put a real door here," he says. "This isn't working."

"That's hundred-year-old heart pine. We are not taking it out. And it works fine. You just have to show it a little love."

"I still don't know how I let you talk me into this place."

I turn and flip my skirt up over my ass.

"Oh, yeah." He zips his suitcase. "If we didn't live two hours outside Nashville, we wouldn't have to pack a bag to go to a show."

"It's barely an hour and a half. And you love spending a few days in the city."

"I love you. That's why I make these sacrifices."

"And I love you. But I also love this house."

"Sometimes, I think you might love it more."

"Aw, sweetie. I love you both the same." I spin around, hoping he's paying more attention to me than the creak of our old hardwood floors. "Do these boots look okay with this outfit or should I change?"

"You look amazing. Are you ready?"

"I've been ready. I was just waiting on you."

Even with valet parking and VIP tickets, we barely make it to our seats before the lights go down.

He takes the stage like he was born to be there, and the crowd goes wild when he steps up to the mic.

"Hello, Nashville! Thank y'all for coming out tonight. And special thanks to special friends who made this life happen for me."

His eyes find us, and Law nods discreetly. I bounce on my toes, blow him a kiss, and wave. The fact that Derringer acknowledges us like that at the opening of every show we attend is testament to his character. He was always good. He just needed to find his people.

We all did.

I still get chills when his voice resonates from the stage.

"I'm from a long line of tall men with loud mouths
They say loyalty matters and blood is the glue,
But all that's left in their veins is..."

The whole arena joins in to shout, "That west Texas crude!"

Law squeezes my hand, and the smile on his face tells me everything I need to know. We're going to have a great weekend in Nashville. Derringer's show tonight, the Astros game in his favorite sports bar tomorrow...

By Monday, when I tell him I'm ready to renovate the barn, he'll be in a much better place to hear it. He'll balk about it until it's underway, and he'll complain until it's done, but he's going to love that recording studio.

Thank you for reading Greta and Law's story! Don't miss the other books in the Rocky Start Romance series:

Changed Plan:
"Get to the airport early," they say. "You don't want to miss your flight."

I got here three hours before my departure time. But my flight decided to miss me.

Everyone's flight has been canceled.

They can't all have weather delays!

All I want is to roast on a beach in Florida and forget all about the fact that I've been fired.

The last thing I need is this human-shaped Golden Retriever, who won't stop smiling at me and telling me it's not so bad. I don't know what I did to attract this man. Was it my entirely unapproachable expression? The way I was screaming at customer service on my phone? Whatever the reason, I am not sharing a hotel room with him.

His snores probably come out in the tune of "You Are My Sunshine."

Not only does he get on my last nerve, but I don't trust him. He's too happy to be real. Even if he does seem genuinely interested in helping me find some joy in spite of my current situation.

It's not like letting him make me smile is going to change anything.

Locked Door:
One of us has definitely gotten our dates wrong. And it's definitely not me.

If there's one thing I'm good at, it's planning and keeping things organized. Okay, that's two things, but they're related, and they are the most crucial aspects of who I am.

I am a professional organizer.

Who cares if that national brand didn't want to partner with me, and those TV star entrepreneurs said "no deal?" Their loss.

I'm not escaping to this vacation rental to lick my wounds from my recent rejections. I just need a quiet place to regroup and plan my next move. To organize my thoughts.

And I'm very sorry for this seemingly nice guy, who has misunderstood that this house is his for the week.

Okay, so it appears I made a teeny error in my calendar.

But I'm not about to make another mistake and spend a week in a house with a total stranger. Even if he is a complete mess, who could seriously use my help.

It's not like he could help me in any way.

My website is the best place to see all my books as well as sign up

for my newsletter, where you can find out about upcoming books, signing events, and all my other bookish news!
https://indiesparks.net

Made in the USA
Monee, IL
20 May 2025